THE FIREMAN IN UNIT C

LEE SWIFT

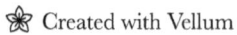 Created with Vellum

Acknowledgments

This one is for Chadrick Douglas and Mike C.

I'm so lucky to have such wonderful and talented friends.

Mockingbird Place

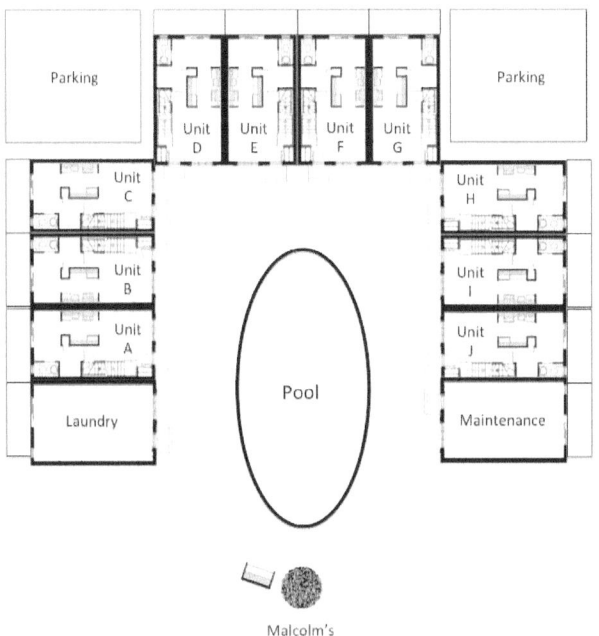

Parking

Unit D Unit E Unit F Unit G

Parking

Unit C

Unit H

Unit B

Unit I

Unit A

Unit J

Pool

Laundry

Maintenance

Malcolm's
Tree

<table>
<tr><td>Chapter 1</td></tr>
</table>

*J*ackson McAllen – Unit D

AFTER SPENDING several hours at the university's library studying for my forensic psychology test next week, I drive away from the campus, anxious to get into my apartment and warm bed. Though I love the class, the amount of required reading has kept me very busy.

Thankfully, I don't have any classes on Fridays this semester, so I can sleep in tomorrow. I'll need the rest for Saturday's tennis match. The new coach doesn't believe in canceling no matter the weather. I really hope the forecast for the weekend is correct. We're supposed to have clear skies and temperatures in the sixties. That will be a relief since this entire week has been so cold, especially today, which is the coldest.

The car is registering the outside temperature at ten degrees below freezing. It gives me a chill just looking at it.

I pull into my parking space at Mockingbird Place, my home sweet home. Bracing myself to face the cold, I open my car door and immediately smell smoke.

I look around and see where it's coming from. Shit. It's Eli's apartment.

God, I hope he's at the fire station working and not inside.

I call 9-1-1.

The dispatcher answers, "9-1-1. What's your emergency?"

"I'm reporting a fire at Mockingbird Place." I give her the address. "Unit C. I'm going to run to the door and make sure no one is inside."

"Sir, for your safety you need to wait until the fire department gets there," she says in a stern voice.

As I'm running, I tell her, "No way am I waiting." At Eli's door, I try to turn the knob. It's locked. I pound as hard as I can. "Eli! Eli! Are you in there?"

My neighbors come out of their apartments. More smoke billows out the front window. I see that it's broken. This could be arson. That realization multiplies my worry. Where the hell are you, Eli?

"I know I'm not supposed to hang up on you, ma'am, but I have to call my friend to make sure he's okay." Not waiting for her to respond, I click off of 9-1-1 and call Eli's phone.

Sirens begin to wail in the distance.

Fuck. No answer.

Out of the corner of my eye I see something move. Hoping that it's Eli, I turn and see the white stray cat that we've all adopted running down the sidewalk.

I knock even louder. "Eli!"

Suddenly, the door opens, releasing a massive amount of smoke. Eli rushes out with a towel around his waist and another covering his mouth.

"Eli, are you okay?"

Coughing, he puts his arms around me. "Yes, I am."

I'm overwhelmed with relief that he is safe, but I'm feeling so much more that I can't explain. There's no time to sort out these thoughts right now.

Eli coughs a few more times and then his demeanor goes into fireman mode. "Jackson, we need to step away from the building. It's too dangerous. Please help me get everyone back." He doesn't wait for me but begins lifting his hands and motioning everyone to the other side of the pool. Following his lead, I do the same, directing our neighbors away from the fire.

Once he's satisfied that everyone is safely away from the blaze, I take off my coat and give it to him. Then he and I run around to the back of Mockingbird Place and meet a fire truck, an ambulance, and a police car, which are pulling into the parking lot next to our units.

The firemen jump out and get to work like a well-oiled machine, pulling out the hoses and other equipment.

Still coughing, Eli steps over to the man in charge, who is broad shouldered with salt and pepper hair.

"Grayson? What the hell are you doing here wrapped in a towel?" the man asks.

"It's my place, Captain," Eli chokes out. "I was in the shower when I heard glass breaking and smelled gasoline. I ran downstairs and saw my sofa and curtains go up in flames. I grabbed my fire extinguisher from under the kitchen sink and tried to put out the blaze but it was already out of control."

"Damn arsonists. This is the fifth fire we've had to deal with in the past two weeks."

I curl my hands into fists, angry about the attacks on gays that have occurred in the area. First it started out as bashing. Eleven LGBT people ended up in the hospital. After the police increased their presence down on Cedar Springs, that's when small apartment complexes around the area, like ours, were set on fire. Although there has been no evidence connecting the bashings to the arsons, the entire community is on edge.

The captain motions to the EMTs to come over. "He's one of ours. Inhaled some smoke. Take good care of him." He turns to Eli. "We are getting this under control. You know the drill. Stay put."

"Yes, sir."

As the EMTs give Eli oxygen and provide him blankets, the captain and his team put out the blaze.

"I'm fine, fellas." Eli seems far from fine to me, at least not emotionally, which is no surprise considering all he's gone through.

Even so, he's still the perfect example of male beauty. He's six-foot-one, just like me. Muscles for days. Piercing blue eyes. Thick, dark hair. Just like the old cliché says—tall, dark, and handsome. He looks like a very strong, tough guy, but still, who would be fine after their home caught on fire? I hate that this has happened to him.

A little while later, the captain walks over to us. "Eli, the good news is we were able to keep the fire from spreading to your second floor. The bad news is everything in your living room is toast. And you know the kind of water damage you're going to have to deal with."

"Yes, sir." He sighs. "And the smoke damage too. The adjoining unit has a couple who are expecting a baby. I'm going to need help finding them a place to stay. Lashaya can't take a chance breathing in the residual smoke."

"You may be jumping the gun," I tell him. I know how terrific a guy Eli is—always concerned about everyone else more than himself. "There might not be any smoke in their place. If there is, we'll all work on getting them settled until it's safe for her to return to their apartment."

He nods. "I'm just glad no one got hurt."

"We did find the remains of what looks to be a Molotov cocktail in the middle of your apartment," the captain says. "Before you can get inside the investigators will have to go over your place first."

Eli closes his eyes. "Maybe they'll find a clue to who did this."

Of course he's still struggling with what has happened. Who wouldn't be?

"I'm sorry but you're not going to be able to stay here." The captain puts his arm around him. "You can stay at the station until this gets all sorted out. I know it might be hard to get much rest but at least you'll have a clean bed and a shower."

Everything inside me wants to help Eli. "Why don't you stay with me? I have the extra bedroom now that Trace is living with Luke, Ava, and the baby. And you and I are about the same size. I have plenty of clothes you can wear." I don't want him to think I'm only offering as a gesture of charity, so I add, "And quite frankly, I could use the company. I've been a little lonely since Trace moved out."

"Are you sure?"

"Of course I am. The first thing we need to do is get you out of the cold."

He shakes his head. "I'd rather stay here until the fire is completely out."

Knowing I would feel the same way if it were my place on fire, I nod. "Okay. But I'm going to get something for your bare feet. I'll be right back."

I run into my place and up the stairs. I pull out a pair of slippers from my closet.

As I rush back to Eli, I see the fire is already under control. The captain is talking with two police officers, a male and female. I also spot Sarah and Martha, who we lovingly call S & M, giving the firemen coffee and hot chocolate.

I hand the slippers to Eli. "I hope these fit you."

"My feet feel like icicles. Thanks, Jackson." Putting them on, he smiles. "Perfect, buddy. Already feel better. But let me give your coat back. You must be freezing too."

I was so concerned with getting him the slippers I didn't think about grabbing a coat for myself. "I'm fine. Keep it, Eli."

The captain leads the police officers to us. "This is Eli Grayson. Eli, they have a few questions they need to ask you."

"I'm Detective Soliz," the female officer says, and then motions to her partner. "And this is Detective Morrison."

I recall what the outside temperature registered on my car earlier. *Ten degrees below freezing.* "Officers, I know you have to ask him questions but could we please go inside my place so he can warm up?" I point to my back door. "I live next door to him."

Soliz nods. "Of course. Lead the way."

Once we're all settled into my apartment, I turn up the heat and put on a pot of coffee. I wish my friend Detective Derek Stone could take Eli's statement. But Derek only works homicides.

"Mr. Grayson, I understand Captain Murphy told you about his suspicions that this could be arson," Soliz says.

"Yes he did."

"Do you have any idea who might have done this?"

"No. I don't have any enemies that I know of."

Morrison asks, "Have you had an argument with anyone recently?"

Eli shrugs. "I did have an argument with my friend Scott a couple of days ago, but that's not unusual. We've been arguing with each other since I kicked him out, but I'm certain Scott's not capable of this."

Of course the bastard is capable of this and so much more. Why can't Eli see the guy for who he truly is?

Soliz looks directly at Eli. "What were you arguing about, Mr. Grayson?"

"Same old thing. He wants me to forgive him and take him back."

We all know the asshole cheated on him, even if Eli has never said so. I saw Scott making out with a guy at a club when he was still living with Eli. And despite Eli breaking it off with the bastard and kicking him out, the creep somehow is able to make Eli feel sorry for him.

I bring out a tray with coffee, cups, cream, and sugar. "Officers, would you like some coffee? It's freezing out there."

"I sure would," Morrison says.

Soliz smiles. "Me, too. Thank you."

"What about you, Eli?" I ask him.

"Please. I'm still cold."

After taking a sip of coffee, Soliz turns back to Eli. "What's your friend's full name, Mr. Grayson?"

"Scott Foster."

"Do you have his address and phone number?" she asks.

"I do. In my cell." Eli frowns. "Oh shit. It was on the table next to my sofa. Um…Scott lives in a condo on Cedar Springs not far from Oak Lawn. I think they're called Whispering Pines."

"Whispering Pines?" I'm stunned. "Those are really nice."

"Where does Mr. Foster work?" Soliz asks Eli.

"He just started working part time at the 7-Eleven on Lemmon a couple of weeks ago."

I wonder how in the hell his ex can afford to live in an upscale condo. Is Eli subsidizing him?

Eli takes a sip of his coffee. "But like I said before, Scott isn't capable of such a crime."

"But he certainly is a big jerk," I blurt out and immediately wish I could take it back. "Sorry, Eli. You know none of us here like Scott after all he did to you."

"What is your name?" Soliz asks me.

Damn it. I should have kept my mouth shut. "Jackson McAllen.

"What can you tell us about Mr. Foster?"

"I don't really know him. I only saw him a few times when he and Eli were still together."

She leans forward. "And?"

"And I don't care for him."

"Can you elaborate?" Morrison asks in a I-mean-business-so-don't-try-to-bullshit-me tone.

"I've seen him throw a drink in Eli's face, scream at Eli at a club, and throw Eli's clothes in the pool." Rage rolls up inside me. Why can't Eli see his ex is a useless piece of shit? "Scott Foster is a total asshole."

Soliz glances at her partner and then turns back to me. "Are you and Mr. Grayson dating now?"

"No, we are not," Eli jumps in. "Jackson and I are only friends."

His words sting me. "Right. Just friends."

"I don't understand why you're wasting time, officers," Eli says. "Stop trying to pin this on Scott. I told you, he's not capable of this."

The male officer's eyebrows rise. "Have you heard the saying from Hamlet 'The lady doth protest too much, methinks'?"

Is Morrison referring to Eli's ex being the arsonist or that Eli and I should be together? God, I wish Eli and I could be more than friends. I like him. I like him a lot. But he and I wouldn't work. His life is too complicated and messy for me. Blame it on my OCD. I must have things simple and orderly.

Chapter 2

S ince Eli is still shivering, I pour him another cup of coffee.

"Thanks, buddy," he says.

The two officers who took his statement left over an hour ago. That's when all our neighbors came into my place to give Eli their support.

"Anyone else?" I ask.

"None for me." Trace holds a sleeping little Mick in his arms. He turns to his new husband Luke and Ava, who is the baby's mother and lives with them. "In fact, we better get going. It's late."

"What time is it?" Eli asks.

"Past one in the morning. Time for all of us to say goodnight," Martha states loudly. "Eli, when you get up tomorrow give S and I a call. We'll gather the troops and start sorting out your things."

He smiles. "I will. Thank all of you. It means the world to me that you are here."

She kisses him on the cheek and everyone leaves my apartment.

Now Eli and I are alone.

With shaking hands he brings the cup of coffee to his lips. "God, this is just what I needed, Jackson."

"You're still cold?"

He nods. "Yes, I am. I can't seem to get warm. This reminds me of something my grandmother says. 'I'm chilled to the bone.' "

"I know what you need. Follow me." I lead him upstairs to the bathroom. "A hot shower will do the trick. I'll get you some clothes and a robe." I hand him a towel, washcloth, and a new toothbrush.

"You're prepared for anything, aren't you?"

"It's part of my OCD. You know the old saying—hope for the best but prepare for the worst. I bet your grandmother says that too."

"She sure does. She's big on sayings." He sighs. "This is one of the worst things I've ever faced."

That's saying a lot since he risks his life putting out fires.

"Eli, you heard what Martha said. Everyone at Mockingbird Place is here for you. Don't forget, we are family." I place my hand on his shoulder. "I'm here for you, too. You're not alone in this."

"All I can say is thank you." He wraps his arms around me, holding me for several seconds.

God, I like the feel of him. Warmth spreads through my body. *I can't let myself feel this way.* Eli and me? That can never happen. But I have to admit I've been attracted to him for a very long time. If I let my guard down we will end up in a total mess. So the only way we can remain friends is for me to keep my feelings in check. But shit, they're already taking control.

Trying to engage my willpower, I step back. "Let me get you some clothes."

"Great."

I watch him bend over and turn on the water.

As fast as I can, I walk out of the room.

I shouldn't be looking at him this way. His home just burned for crying out loud.

When I return with the promised clothes and robe, he's leaning over the sink brushing his teeth in nothing but a damn towel. My God, he's so hot. I just can't help but look at him.

"Here you go." I hand him the clothes and hurry down the stairs. I have to get away before I do something I'll regret.

I hear him yell, "Thanks again. For everything."

Damn, I wish I could give him everything. My heart is racing in my chest. What's wrong with me? *Get a hold of yourself, Jackson.*

When I hear the shower turn on, I take a deep breath. Needing something to distract myself from visualizing what's happening upstairs in my bathroom—a hot fireman washing his naked body—I decide my kitchen floor could use a good mopping.

When I'm halfway finished with the job, Eli walks into the kitchen wearing my robe. That does it. I'll never be able to put on that robe again without remembering this very moment with his hot body inside it.

He smiles. "Trace told me about your late night chores, but I had no idea you worked this *late*. Need some help, Jackson?"

"No thanks. Just burning off some energy."

"By mopping? At two in the morning? Are you sure there's not something on your mind?"

"No. I'm just keyed up after the fire." It's part of the truth. The other part of the truth—where I want to rip that robe off of him and make love until the sun comes up? That part needs to stay a secret. "I know it's silly, but cleaning helps me relax."

"It's not silly. I eat to burn off energy. Guys at the station say I have a bottomless pit for a stomach. And boy, could I use a big thick cheeseburger or a stack of pancakes from Aunt Lucy's Diner right now."

"I bet you could. I'm hungry too. Instead of going out, why don't I make us something to eat here? I've got eggs and bacon. Once our stomachs are full I'm sure we'll be able to fall right to sleep."

He grins. "Sounds great."

Seeing his gorgeous smile causes a wave of tingles to roll through me. "I'll get started as soon as the floor dries. It shouldn't take but a few minutes."

"That will work just fine."

I put the mop away.

"Jackson, I actually came down to see if you had a razor and shaving cream I could borrow."

"I sure do. Follow me."

We go upstairs into the bathroom, and I see he's left a towel on the floor. I take a deep breath, forcing my OCD down. *It's only a towel.*

When Trace lived with me he was always doing the same thing. I never bit my tongue then.

But I wasn't having these kinds of feelings for Trace.

I pick up the towel and hang it on the rod, reminding myself why it would be impossible for Eli and me to be together.

"I'm sorry, Jackson. It must have fallen off the hook. I'll be more careful next time."

"No worries." He did hang up the towel. It just fell. *Maybe not so impossible after all.*

I glance at the hook on the back of the door. I never hang towels from it, only my robe, but he had no idea about that. I was wrong about him. But that really doesn't change the fact that he's still tied up with his ex.

Opening the cabinet, I pull out a new razor and can of shaving cream. "Will these do?"

"Perfect. Thanks. Where would I be without you tonight, Jackson?"

"I'm glad you're here with me," I confess. Quickly, I add, "Any one of our neighbors would have done the same thing. I just wish I'd seen the prick who threw the Molotov cocktail through your window."

"Me, too. I have another favor to ask you."

"Sure. What is it?"

"I know everyone will be showing up at my place fairly early tomorrow, I mean today." He laughs. "I look for S & M to be the first on the scene, probably eight at the latest."

"I think you're right. Everyone else will show up by nine or ten."

"I really want to go into my apartment before the rest of them arrive. That may sound crazy, especially since I'm with the fire department."

"Not crazy at all. It makes perfect sense that you would want to inspect your place alone."

"Well, not actually alone. Would you mind getting up early so we can beat everyone there?"

"I don't mind at all." I'm thrilled he wants me there with him. "What time do you want me to set the alarm?"

"Six, but I'll probably wake up before then. Fireman habit. I really appreciate this, Jackson."

"It's no big deal, and it's my pleasure." I have the oddest urge to hug him but I don't. "You finish cleaning up and I'll get our food ready."

As I descend the stairs, my doorbell rings.

"Who in the hell could that be at this hour?" I open the door and find the last person on earth I want to see. "What are you doing here, Scott?"

Eli's ex's eyes narrow. "I'm here for my boyfriend."

Boyfriend? This guy won't give up.

"I came the minute I got off work." The white stray cat comes up beside him. "Who's this pretty thing?"

Even though I don't feel like small talk I still answer. "Everyone is calling her Snow. She just started showing up a few days ago."

Scott bends down to pet her, but the cat scurries off before he can. Could Scott have some redeemable qualities that I've been missing? Eli had to have seen something in Scott to date him.

"Still too skittish I see. Keep feeding her and she'll be sitting in your laps before too long." Standing up, he looks me in the eye. "Eli is here with you, right?"

I feel my insides tighten. I don't trust this guy, not one damn bit. There is something eerie in his eyes. Or is it just my imagination? "How do you know Eli is here?"

"One of your neighbors told me," he states flatly.

I can't imagine anybody at Mockingbird Place telling Scott where he is. They know the bad history between the two of them as well as I do. "That doesn't answer my first question. Why are you here?"

"The fire, of course."

God, I don't trust a word that comes out of his mouth. "How did you hear about the fire?"

"The police scanner." Scott's face darkens and he closes his eyes. "It's a habit I started when my brother became a fireman. I've kept it up even though he died."

I'm no fool. Scott's trying to evoke sympathy from me like he does with Eli, but it's not going to work. I hate that Scott lost his brother, but I also hate how he uses that tragedy to manipulate Eli. "Eli told me about your brother. They were good friends. When he died in that four-alarm fire it tore Eli up."

"It tore me up, too. Did you know that my brother is the one who introduced Eli and me?"

I'm shocked. Is it true or just another tactic the jerk is trying on me? "No. I didn't know that."

Eli's ex smiles at me in a way that seems so condescending. Scott thinks he has the upper hand now. "Jackson, isn't it?"

"You know it is." I smell liquor on his breath. "Are you drunk?"

"No. I just had one drink."

I stand with my hands on the door and its frame, blocking him from coming in. Maybe Eli is right about Scott not starting the fire, but the creep is definitely up to no good. He's the last person Eli needs to see tonight. "If you care anything at all about Eli, you'll let him get some rest."

"I just want to let Eli know that I'm here for him."

"I'll be sure to tell him you came by."

As I start to close the door, Scott steps forward, putting his hand on it. "I'm not leaving until I see Eli."

I glare at him. "Oh really?"

Before I can slam the door in the bastard's face, Eli comes down the stairs. "Scott? What are you doing here?"

Shoving me out of the way, Scott rushes inside and grabs Eli. "Oh my God, I heard about the fire on the scanner. I was afraid I'd lost you like I lost my brother. What would I have done if you had been hurt or worse?"

Scott's melodramatic outburst sickens me. He's laying it on so thick. He just wants to get on Eli's good side.

"I'm fine." Eli smiles. "I can't say the same for my sofa though."

I wonder if he's buying into Scott's act. It seems like he might be. Surely Eli can see through Scott's performance for what it is—just a way to manipulate him.

"Knowing what you went through breaks my heart." Scott stares at Eli. "I should have been there with you."

"That wouldn't have changed anything. It was arson."

"Arson? How do you know it was arson?"

"Someone threw a Molotov cocktail through Eli's window." I stare at him hoping to see any sign that will tell me if he is the one responsible.

The asshole's eyes widen. "Do the police have any clue who could have done this?"

"Not yet, but they're just starting their investigation," Eli says.

"This is so awful. I wish this had never happened. It brings back all the horrible memories."

God, Scott is such a bullshit artist. His overreaction gives the impression he might be innocent. I'm not positive he's the one behind the fire, but the way he's acting makes me suspicious. Until I know for certain who is guilty I will be keeping my eye on Eli's ex.

"I bet it's the same people who have been burning down places in Oak Lawn." Scott frowns. "I need to get you out of this area. It's too dangerous. My place is much safer. It's gated and we have an on-site security guard."

"I'm not waving the white flag to a homophobe and neither is our community. The police will find the person responsible for these attacks."

"Or *persons*," Scott says. "It might be a gang."

"Maybe so, but usually arsonists act alone. Don't worry about me, Scott. Jackson has been great. I'm so thankful he's letting me stay here until I can get back in my place."

"But that's why I'm here, honey," Scott says in a sticky sweet tone, making me wish I could rip his tongue right out of his mouth. "You need to come home with me. You'll be much more comfortable in my apartment than you could ever be here. I know exactly what you like and need."

It takes every bit of my willpower not to slam the fucker to the floor. I turn to Eli, praying he will come to his senses about his ex. *Eli, wake up. Open your eyes. See what a bastard Scott is.*

But when he puts his hands on Scott's shoulders, I realize Eli is still blind to Scott's antics.

"I appreciate the offer," he says. "But since Jackson is willing to let me stay here that's what I'm going to do."

"But, Eli—"

"You heard the man, Scott. He wants to stay here." Realizing I might have overstepped, I add, "Besides, it's next door to his place so it will be easy for him to check on everything."

Scott glares at me. "Stay out of this, asshole. It's none of your business."

"Stop it." Eli takes a step back from the creep. "I think it's time for you to leave. We'll talk later."

"Honey, I'm sorry."

"Stop calling me honey," Eli says firmly.

"I'm just so upset." Scott turns to me. "Jackson, I know you mean well. I shouldn't have exploded like that. You're a good friend to Eli. I'm so glad."

Seeing through the bastard's charade, I say, "Yeah, I'm sure you are."

For a split second Scott's warm demeanor turns icy. Shining through his eyes is an intense anger. But just as fast as it appeared it vanishes, and the false expression he's been showing since Eli came down the stairs returns.

With a pleading look, Scott turns back to him. "Please, Eli. Come home with me. I can bring you back first thing in the morning and we can get to work on cleaning your place."

"No, Scott. I'm staying. Please, just go home now."

"Okay, sweetheart, I'll go. I know you're dealing with a lot of emotions. Fires can ruin people's entire lives." Scott sighs. "Like a fire did mine when it took my brother."

Oh, for crying out loud, this guy won't stop trying to get under Eli's skin. I'm so over it.

"It's time for you to leave, Scott." I grab him by the arm and lead him to the door, away from Eli.

Scott continues his performance, smiling broadly. "Whatever you need, honey, I will do. You know how much you mean to me."

"Then go home, Scott. Goodnight." Eli walks back upstairs, obviously frustrated.

It's clear that the early morning meal we were going to share isn't going to happen, thanks to his ex's unexpected arrival.

Scott steps outside, and in a very low tone says, "You haven't seen the last of me, motherfucker."

He storms off.

As I shut the door, I wonder what Eli ever saw in that prick.

Chapter 3

E arly the next morning, I open my bedroom door and get a whiff of bacon, pancakes, and coffee coming up the stairs. It's no surprise that Eli got up before me because he's so anxious to check out the damage at his place. What does surprise me is that he has made breakfast.

When I walk into the kitchen, he greets me with a broad smile. "Good morning."

"Morning." I'm so glad to see him in a better mood than when Scott was here last night.

"Jackson, I hope you don't mind me cooking. I was starving when I woke up this morning." He hands me a cup of coffee.

"Me, too. I had no idea you could cook." I look at the mess he's made but for some strange reason it doesn't bother me—*too much.* "I'm so thrilled you did this for me…for us."

"And don't worry. I'm going to get the dishes put away. When I'm done you won't even know I've been here."

"No, you won't. I won't have you cooking and cleaning both. The rule in this place has always been the one who cooks sits while the other cleans. Just ask Trace. He knows."

"He should. You two lived together for quite some time. I'll make a deal with you. Just this once can we clean it up together? I'm very anxious to get over to my apartment and I want you with me."

"Since you put it that way, it's a deal. But tonight I'm cooking dinner and handling the clean up."

"That will work great." Eli winks at me.

Damn, this man is sexy. How am I going to be able to resist him? Not that I really want to, but I still think it might be for the best. After last night's theatrics with Scott, it's pretty clear that Eli is having trouble making a break. And it's also very clear that Scott has no intention of backing down.

What a mess. I don't need to get in the middle of their crap.

If Eli is finally able to make a break of it, maybe there might be a chance for him and me. Or maybe not? Who knows? Probably just wishful thinking on my part. Either way, until he truly ends things with Scott, we can only be friends. Nothing more. God, that won't be easy, especially since he's sleeping in my apartment right across the hall from me. I've never been this attracted to a guy in my life. Fire or no fire, I want to jump his bones. That's a big problem for me.

Doing the best I can to keep my lust in check, I enjoy the delicious breakfast he made.

"You think Snow would like some leftover bacon?" he asks.

"Not a chance, but I have some cat food I bought the other day for her. We can put it out."

"You and everyone else at Mockingbird Place." He smiles. "She's going to be the fattest cat in the neighborhood if we don't set up a feeding schedule."

I grin. "You don't know that much about cats, do you?"

"Not really. My family had dogs."

An image of my mother surrounded by all the cats she collected enters my mind. I push it away. "Cats are different, especially feral cats. They usually don't overeat."

"That makes me feel better about Snow." He sighs. "Scott has a cat. He's a big animal lover."

Eli mentioning his ex reminds me how attached they still are despite being broken up. Will he ever be able to ends things once and for all with the guy? I hope so.

"The breakfast was delicious." I clear our plates from the table. "If the fireman gig doesn't work out for you, I have no doubt you could open your own restaurant and be very successful."

He wipes off the table. "The fireman gig is working out great, Jackson. If I had to cook professionally day in and day out I would hate it, but I do love cooking for friends and family."

I laugh. "Then I'm certainly glad I'm your friend."

It takes us very little time to get the kitchen back in order, and then we go over to his place.

The broken window is boarded up. Harvey took care of it last night after things settled down. Even though he's in his late-seventies, Harvey is still one of the best maintenance men in the city. We're lucky to have him at Mockingbird Place, especially since he doesn't need the money. He does it because we're family to him and he's family to us.

Eli opens his apartment's door and the smell of smoke is intense. "We better leave this open."

"Yes, and we should open the back door and all the windows, too."

We walk inside, our shoes sloshing on the soaked carpet. The scene is awful. I can taste the remnants of the blaze on my tongue. Ashy and bitter. Every surface is black with wet soot.

Eli's living room furniture is destroyed. His flat screen TV is melted. Everything will have to be replaced. Luckily, it looks like the blaze was contained in the living room and didn't spread to the kitchen or dining room, though both suffered smoke and water damage.

Even though it's obvious that Eli can see the extent of the loss, his entire focus is on a burnt basket of laundry in the middle of the room.

"Damn it." He starts pulling out the ruined clothing with bits of the basket's plastic stuck to each piece, tossing them to the floor.

I can tell he's about to lose it. "We can replace these clothes."

"This can't be replaced, Jackson. I have to find it."

"Okay. Okay. I'll help you." I kneel down next to him, organizing the damaged articles he's discarded into a pile. Falling apart in my hands, I know they're beyond repair. "What are you looking for, Eli?"

"This." The last piece of clothing Eli grabs is the remains of a T-shirt with a few letters on it I can't make out. Clutching it in his fist, he stares at the burnt article. "Fuck, I had planned on doing the laundry after my shower."

I place my hand on his shoulder. "This is obviously something that means a lot to you."

"Jason's mom had it made for me." His gaze never leaves the T-shirt.

I can tell that wrapped up in it are memories for Eli that are powerful and intense. It doesn't matter that it is a fraction of the cost of the other things he's lost. "Who's Jason?"

He turns to me and his grip on the shirt loosens a little. "He's the only baby I've ever delivered. I'd only been at the department for one month. As the new guy, I was assigned the job of keeping the pantry stocked for our station. When I was walking to my car with the groceries, I saw a pregnant woman in the parking lot bent over a cart moaning. I rushed over to her, let her know I was a fireman, and asked if she wanted help. She told me she needed to push. I quickly dialed 9-1-1 and helped her to her car. After she yelled that the baby was coming I knew the EMTs wouldn't arrive in time. Even though I'd never done anything like that in my life, my training kicked in.

"It was a miracle, Jackson. I'm crazy about that little boy. Jason is two years old now. He calls me Unkey Lee-Lee. That's what was on this shirt that his mom, Elisa, gave me." Eli's eyes well up. "I know everything else can be replaced, but this can't."

I put my arms around him, hoping in some small way to help him feel better.

Eli hugs me back, and then to my surprise, he kisses me.

"Get your fucking lips off of him, asshole." Scott rushes in and grabs my arm, trying to pry us apart. "Who the hell do you think you are? Eli is mine."

"I'm not yours, Scott. I've never been yours." Eli glares at the creep as S & M come through the front door with a man I don't recognize. "Let go of Jackson. Now."

Releasing my arm, Scott changes his tune, clearly because we now have an audience. "I'm sorry. I thought he was taking advantage of you."

"Bullshit," I say flatly, though I'm still reeling from Eli's kiss. Why did he kiss me? I didn't have time to really think about it since Scott interrupted us.

Eli stands in front of Scott. "Get out."

"But I brought donuts. I'm sorry, sweetheart. It's just seeing your place like this is tough for me. It takes me back. I can't help but think about my brother."

"Not that again," I blurt out.

"What the fuck does that mean?" Scott shoves a white box into my chest. "You don't even know me, Jackson. I came with donuts for everyone, hoping to help my man get his place back in order. What do I find? You trying to get your claws into him. Fuck you."

Eli moves between us. "Go. Now. Get out, Scott. I won't say it again."

The bastard holds his ground. "Honey, please. We just need to—"

"Damn it, Scott. Stop calling me honey. I won't say it again." Eli's face is bright red. Once again his ex has pushed this laid-back, wonderful man over the edge. "Get the fuck out of my house or I'll throw your ass out. And take your damn donuts with you."

"You're making a big mistake." Scott turns to me. "A very big mistake. You don't know who you're dealing with."

The man with S & M says, "Just who are we dealing with?"

"Who wants to know?" Scott snaps back.

"Officer Reagan with the Dallas Fire Department. I'm the investigator on this case."

Scott quickly steps over to the man and shakes his hand. Once again his demeanor switches to a less aggressive state. "Nice to meet you. I'm Scott Foster. My brother was with the department. Kevin Foster. He was killed last year in the line of duty. Did you know him, Officer Reagan?"

"I knew of him but I never met him. Right now, I have some questions for you, Mr. Foster. Since you've been asked to leave I think we should do them outside."

"Sure thing, sir," Scott says with a smile and steps out of the apartment.

Before Officer Reagan follows him, he says, "Which one of you is Eli Grayson?"

"I am, sir."

"I read the statement that you gave to the police, but I would like to interview you myself."

"Of course. Whatever you need from me to help with your investigation I'm glad to give. I will be here most of the day. Whenever it's convenient for you that will work for me."

"Excellent. How about when I finish with Mr. Foster?"

Eli nods. "Sure."

The man walks out the door to join Scott.

Martha sighs. "My goodness, Eli, that friend of yours seems very troubled."

"He is. Very."

That's putting it mildly.

"Well, let's get to work," Martha says. "We've already let everyone know that the washers and dryers are yours alone until we get all your things cleaned. Are you okay with S and I gathering up your clothes and linens to get the laundry started?"

"That would be great."

Sarah gives Eli a hug. "We've also contacted the insurance company."

"I know," he says. "My agent called me last night, and she's sending an adjuster to work my claim as well as the complex's. He's supposed to be here between now and noon."

"Speak of the Devil," Martha says. "I think that may be him walking up the sidewalk."

When the man gets to the door, he hands his card to Eli. "Hello. I'm Thomas Lake with Allied McLemore Insurance."

Eli shakes his hand. "I'm Eli Grayson and these ladies are the owners of Mockingbird Place—Sarah Barnett and Martha Rivers. And this is my friend and next door neighbor, Jackson McAllen. Come on in, sir."

"If we knew you were coming we'd have baked a cake," Sarah says with a grin.

Mr. Lake's eyes narrow. "What? That wouldn't have been necessary."

Martha giggles. "S, these young people don't know that old song."

"Well, they should."

I laugh. "I know it, and I'm young."

"That's only because S and I have sang it at several of our parties, Jackson. No one your age outside of Mockingbird Place would have a clue about it. No wonder Mr. Lake is confused."

The adjuster smiles. "I'm not that young, ma'am, and now that you mention it, I remember my grandmother singing that song whenever she baked. Anyway, is this a good time?"

"It's the perfect time," Eli says.

As Mr. Lake walks around the apartment with Eli and S & M, I step outside to give them more space to work. Remaining on Eli's front steps I see Officer Reagan and Scott sitting on the bench. Whatever the investigator is asking Scott seems to be making him squirm.

I wonder why. Probably because the investigator doesn't care for Scott any more than I do. Or maybe Scott is the guilty party who started the fire. I hope we find out very soon.

"Hey, Jackson." Stephen Norelli, our newest resident, walks up to me.

"Hi Father," I say out of respect.

He grins. "Come on, Jackson. You know I want you to call me Stephen."

"Okay, Stephen. I'll try to remember." I learned he was an Episcopal priest the day he moved in. I had no idea priests could be so young. Stephen is just two years older than I am.

"Where's Eli?" he asks.

"He's inside with S & M and the insurance adjuster. Once they finish we're diving in to clean up the place."

I see more of our neighbors arriving to help, gathering around Eli's door. I notice that Tony is sporting two black eyes and a cut on his chin, which doesn't surprise me.

"Anthony, are you okay?" Stephen asks him, his face full of concern.

"I'm fine," our resident MMA fighter answers flatly. "Had a match last night. That's all. You should see the other guy. I came home with the win. That fucking homophobe ended up with a broken jaw. I mean *f'ing* homophobe. Sorry Father...I mean Stephen. But you are a man of the cloth."

"Yes, I am, but that doesn't make me any more special than anyone else, including you, Anthony." Stephen smiles. "We're all God's children. But please just call me Stephen."

"I'll try, and I promise to watch my language from now on."

Tony trying to keep his language in check shocks me. Even around S & M he's dropped an f-bomb accidently. When they're absent, he just lets them fly. But I have noticed a slight change in his language ever since Stephen moved to Mockingbird Place. Of all the residents here, Tony is the most combative, sullen, and short-tempered person there is. The exact opposite of Father Stephen, who is warm, giving, and never raises his voice.

Stephen has reminded me and everyone else on previous occasions to not be too quick to judge Tony. He believes there's likely more to his story than any of us know. He's probably right. And Tony isn't all bad. He's always one of the first to show up to lend a hand when it's needed. Even so, I can't figure him out despite all the psychology classes I've taken. Am I crazy to think I could be a psychologist one day?

After the adjuster leaves Eli waves us back inside. "I'm so grateful the cavalry has arrived. Thanks, everyone. The good news is the insurance company will be paying for a professional cleaning crew to deal with the water and smoke damage. I would just like to go through my stuff before they show up."

"That's why we're here," Stephen says.

Thinking about my kiss with Eli, I can't take my eyes off of him. Damn Scott for interrupting us. I'm acting like a lovesick teenager. What's wrong with me? Probably the only reason Eli kissed me was because he was so emotional at the time.

Before we have a chance to get started, S & M come down the stairs with their arms full of Eli's smoky clothes. "Tony, do you mind getting the rest of Eli's clothes from the closets and bringing them to the laundry room?"

"Sure thing," Tony says.

"Hold on for a second, Anthony, and I'll help you." Stephen turns to Eli. "I have lunch going for everyone. I have spaghetti, garlic bread, and salad. I also baked a cake for dessert."

S & M, Eli, and I start laughing, remembering the song.

"What's so funny? I can really cook."

"It's not that, Stephen," Eli says, still chuckling. "But it does feel good to laugh." And he explains why it is so funny to the four of us.

"I don't know that song but I can't wait to hear S & M sing it at the next party."

"Why wait?" S & M say in unison, and they burst into song. "If I knew you were coming I'd have baked a cake, baked a cake…" They finish the song and we all clap.

"I've never heard a cuter tune in my whole life," Stephen says.

"Well, that was cute," Eli says, "but my favorite is when they sing 'A bushel and a peck.'"

"I can't wait to hear more."

I grin. "Then you're going to love S & M's next party. They always lead us in a sing-a-long after dessert."

"Let's get the rest of the clothes, Anthony. Then I'll need to get back to my place so I can check on the sauce for the spaghetti. Whenever anyone gets hungry, just come on in. The door will be open. I've got enough for everyone."

"Thanks, Stephen." Eli looks at all of us. "I really appreciate each and every one of you."

When his eyes lock with mine, I feel heat spread throughout me. Damn it. This blows. I can't get involved with him. The best I could hope for would be three months. Maybe six. Then it would be that horrible awkwardness that would follow after the inevitable breakup. And we would be living next door to each other. Awful.

No. I can't let that happen. I won't.

Chapter 4

Eli and I toss his ruined flat screen TV into the dumpster. When it hits the metal container the crash echoes in our ears. Snow, who followed us from Eli's apartment, jumps into my arms.

Eli's eyes are wide with surprise. "Has she ever done that before?"

I shake my head. "She's clearly terrified."

Without warning, Snow jumps out of my arms and runs to the side of the dumpster.

"That was a nice surprise," I say, wiping the bead of sweat from my brow. "Typical Dallas winter. One day below freezing, the next it's almost seventy degrees."

"Plus you're working your ass off to help me." Eli smiles and bends down, trying to coax the cat back. It doesn't take long before she's rubbing up against his boots. "She's getting more tame each day."

"She sure is," I say. "Now we're all fighting over whose house cat she's going to be."

"Why don't you take her in, Jackson?"

His question makes me immediately remember how my mom

was with strays. "No. I can't handle inside pets. But my money is on S & M."

"Mine, too." With a sigh, he glances down in the dumpster. "I only bought this six months ago. What a waste."

Hoping to lift his spirits, I say in my most upbeat tone, "I'm sure the insurance adjuster is going to give you all the money you need to replace this and everything else you lost."

"I know you're right." Another heart-wrenching sigh leaves his lips. "But I'm still having trouble making any sense out of this."

"Eli, there is no *sense* for this. Life sucks sometimes, and this happens to be one of those times."

"Well said, my friend." He steps back from the dumpster and looks directly at me. "When I got up this morning I started wondering if this was or wasn't a random attack. Could it be possible that someone actually wants to hurt me? I don't think I have any enemies."

"I'm sure the investigation will uncover who did this. It could be related to the attacks in Oak Lawn. Or something else." *Or someone else, like your ex.* "But my suggestion is for you to take things one day at a time."

"You're right, once again. This is a lot harder than I thought." He puts his hand on my shoulder. "It's given me a better perspective of what victims of fire have to go through. I think I'll be even more sensitive the next time I arrive on scene—especially with those who have children."

"I can't imagine how hard your job is, Eli."

"Only on some days. There's not a person in the department, including me, who hasn't been moved by the look of a little girl or boy's face after all their toys have been destroyed. Hell, the stuff I lost doesn't compare with a child's treasures."

He is such a caring and wonderful man. No wonder I'm so attracted to him despite how impossible it is for us to ever be together. That doesn't stop my mind from bringing up images of him naked and in my arms.

Suddenly, Eli's face darkens.

"What's the matter?" I ask.

"Thank God I wasn't taking care of Jason. I might have been if he and his mom weren't visiting family in Iowa this week."

"You take care of the boy often?"

"He spends the night with me when I'm off duty and his mother has to work late. It's tough for Elisa being a single parent, so I try to do what I can to help."

It's clear to me how much he cares for the little boy and his mom. "You're a good person, Eli—a good friend."

"So are you, Jackson. So are you." He points at the back of his apartment. "God, if Jason had been with me it might have caused him to have nightmares. Or what if he'd been hurt. I would have never been able to forgive myself."

Seeing him struggle with the what-might-have-been, I look Eli directly in the eyes. "That little boy wasn't hurt and he wasn't with you. You just told me that Jason is in Iowa with his mom. He is safe and doing just fine, right?"

The tension in his face slowly vanishes and is replaced with a warm smile. "Thanks, Jackson. You know just what to say to make me feel better."

Feeling my stomach rumble, I look at the time on my phone. "Eli, it's almost two and neither of us have had a bite of food since this morning. Let's take a break and head over to Father Stephen's for some of his spaghetti."

"I'm starving. I love that idea, but you better not call him that. You know he likes all of us to just call him Stephen."

Grinning, I say, "I know, but like Tony says, he is a priest after all."

We knock on Unit F's door.

I'm surprised to see Tony answer it.

"You're the last two," he says in his typical surly tone. "I was getting ready to come get you and drag your asses over here to eat."

I laugh. "Thanks, buddy. It's so nice that you care."

"It sure is," Eli says. "We actually forgot to eat."

"Obviously." Tony swings the door wide. The smile that suddenly appears on his face is unusual for him. "Come on in and enjoy the best spaghetti you've ever eaten. Stephen has been keeping everything warm for you."

This is the first time I've been in Unit F since Oliver moved into Unit A with Adam. Oliver has quite the gift in decorating. When he lived here it looked like it could have been featured in a high-design magazine. Not so much now. The apartment is sparse with understated décor. There's a gray sofa and matching chair, a wooden coffee table, a floor lamp and shelves loaded with books. The walls are bare except for a single painting that I immediately recognize as one of Trace's. It's of an eagle in flight over a beautiful lake surrounded by snowcapped mountains. I remember Stephen buying it at Trace's last art show, which was held in Mockingbird Place's courtyard around the pool. The painting is the only thing with color inside the unit. Still, the apartment is inviting and indescribably warm. Why? I can't say.

Stephen walks out of the kitchen wearing a red apron and a wide smile on his face. "Welcome, guys. Have a seat and I'll get your plates ready."

I realize where the warmth is coming from. Stephen is the source of the good feelings of this place. He's our newest resident, but it's like he's lived here his whole life. All of us are already crazy about Father Stephen, the good-looking Episcopal priest.

"What can I get you to drink?" Tony asks. "There's soft drinks, tea, milk or wine. Stephen has both red and white."

I'm a little shocked and curious to see Tony acting as co-host and also doing a great job of it. Very interesting. What's up between these two?

"I could use a glass of red wine." Eli takes a seat on a barstool at Stephen's counter.

"Same for me," I say, moving into the seat next to him.

Stephen begins loading a plate with pasta. "Anthony, grab the bottle of Malbec. You remember where the opener is."

"Yep. The top drawer by the sink."

I look at Eli and he sends me a knowing wink. We're both on the same wavelength. There's definitely something up with Stephen and Tony. What? I'm not sure, but I like the change in the MMA fighter.

Stephen places our plates on the counter.

On two of the plates, one for each of us, are fresh tossed salads with Italian dressing. The other two plates are loaded with delicious smelling spaghetti and a generous slice of French bread.

"Would either of you like Parmesan cheese?" our host asks.

We both tell him yes.

He smiles and grates out some cheese for each of us as Tony hands us our wine glasses.

I take a bite. It's delicious. "This is so good, Stephen. The best Italian food I've ever had."

"Wait." Tony holds up his hands, glancing over at Stephen and then at us. "You need to give thanks for the food."

I've never seen Tony act like this before. Ever. Is he interested in Father Stephen more than just as a friend? I grin. That couldn't be it. Or could it?

"It's okay, Anthony," the charming priest says. "I already prayed over all the food." He chuckles. "Why do you think I've been getting all these compliments? I'm good but I'm not *that good*."

"Your food is amazing." Tony smiles, confusing me even more.

I've only seen him go for the dark, moody guys, like himself. Stephen doesn't fit that profile at all, but I still sense something going on between them. But Stephen is an Episcopalian priest. Do Episcopalian priests take a vow of celibacy like Catholic priests? That's a question I need to find out later. Not now. Not in front Tony. I'm not sure how he would react if I asked Stephen now.

"Go on and eat, guys," Stephen tells Eli and me. "Enjoy your meal. Anthony, how about you and I take a break from the cooking and cleaning and have a glass of wine with them?"

"Definitely." Tony pours each of them a glass while Stephen pulls two chairs over.

"It is so relaxing getting away from the day's chores, Stephen." Eli holds up his glass. "To you, for this great meal and wonderful company."

The four of us clink our glasses together.

The conversation is lively as Eli and I each get seconds of the spaghetti.

"How's it going with your new church?" Eli asks.

Stephen's big smile appears again. "I love it. The people are amazing. Very welcoming, though there are a few who are more conservative than most and aren't thrilled with a gay priest."

I look into his kind eyes and then glance at Tony. No time like the present. *Tony, here it goes, ready or not.* "But, Stephen, does you being gay even matter? You've taken a vow of celibacy, right?"

"No, I haven't. That's not required in the Episcopal Church."

Tony's eyes widen. He clearly didn't know either.

"I remember a promise about cake earlier," I say, hoping to change the subject.

Stephen nods. "There sure is."

We finish the meal off with Stephen's tasty chocolate cake and hot Brazilian coffee. It's the most fun I can remember having in a very long time. Since my mother's death it's been tough to even smile. It took me months to clean up her place. God, how any human being could live in such squalor mystifies me. But she really wasn't living. Not really. Guilt rushes in, threatening to choke me.

"You okay, Jackson?" Eli's question pulls me back to the present.

"Sure. I'm fine." I must have had a funny look on my face that he picked up on. "I was just thinking about something. No big deal."

Thankfully, Eli's phone rings before he can ask me something else. I'm definitely not ready to talk about my mother right now. *Will I ever be ready?*

He looks at the screen. "It's the adjuster, Thomas Lake."

As Eli talks with Mr. Lake, I gather up our empty dishes. "Let me help with the cleanup, Stephen."

"I've got this." Stephen starts loading the dishwasher.

"Jackson is a bit of a neat freak, if you haven't picked up on that yet." Tony moves beside him, and then turns to me. "*We've* got this."

Stephen's grin returns. "He's right. You and Eli need to get some rest. Anthony and I can handle this just fine."

"I agree but try telling Eli that. I'm sure he'll want to go right back to work on his place."

Eli clicks off his phone. "Good news. I'm so glad S & M convinced me to increase my renter's coverage last year. Looks like there will be plenty of money to replace everything I lost in the fire."

"That is great news," I say.

"It sure is." Eli sighs. "Still, I can't wait for the police to find out who did this."

Tony frowns and his eyes darken, which is more typical of his demeanor. "If I find out who's responsible they'll never so much as light a fucking match after I'm done with them."

Stephen puts his hand on Tony's shoulder. "Anthony, breathe."

Tony jerks free of Stephen's touch. "I don't feel like breathing right now."

Maybe I'm wrong about how Tony feels for Stephen.

The fighter's tone rumbles with anger. "Some homophobe asshole or group of assholes attacked my friend. They need to pay." He steps back, clearly lost to his rage. "I need some fresh air." Without another word Tony tosses the cloth he was holding to the counter and storms out.

Stephen, Eli, and I stand in shock for a few moments.

Breaking the silence first, I shake my head. "That was a pretty strong reaction."

"Yeah, but it comes from a place of protectiveness inside him for all of you," Stephen says.

"A place of protectiveness? I don't see that." I shrug. "Sorry, Stephen."

Eli seems just as surprised at Tony's outburst as I am. "But Jackson, he called me his friend."

Stephen nods his head. "Anthony will do anything for his friends. And you *are* his friend, Eli. All of you are."

"I'm trying to wrap my head around the fact that Tony thinks of me that way," Eli says.

"I can only imagine how difficult that might be since Anthony can be a little guarded as well as gruff at times."

"Gruff is putting it mildly," I say.

"Maybe so. But I've seen how he looks at all of you. Like I said

Anthony cares about you, Eli—you and everyone else at Mocking-bird Place."

I'm just as doubtful as Eli is when it comes to our resident MMA fighter. "Stephen, you don't know Tony like we do. He keeps all of us at arms length. Sure, he seems a little closer to S & M, but even with them he is distant."

Stephen smiles. "Even though I've only been here a short time I know him better than you can imagine, Jackson, and the truth is Anthony has a big heart."

I'm starting to get a glimpse of how Stephen sees our bad-tempered neighbor. Have I been reading Tony wrong? "I remember how Tony reacted when he first met Adam—long before Oliver and Adam got married. At the time I thought Tony was being a jerk. After hearing what you just said, I think Tony may have been trying to protect a friend from being hurt. None of us really knew that much about Adam when he first moved into Unit A."

"Anthony's tactics may be rough but he has good intentions."

"I'm still not fully convinced. If Tony thinks of Eli, me, and everyone else as friends, he sure has a strange way of showing it."

Eli puts his hand on my shoulder. "You have to admit what Stephen is saying makes sense. Maybe we should consider trying to be more understanding with Tony. There's more to all of us under the surface."

"Perhaps." I'm so impressed with Eli's sensitivity not only to Tony but also to Scott. But could his undying kindness be the reason he can't shove Scott to the curb? Probably. "But sometimes a lost cause is just that. Lost." All this talk is reminding me of losing my mother, and that makes the guilt start to bubble up inside me—exactly what I don't want to happen, especially now.

"Jackson, who knows what caused Tony to close himself off from the world?"

"I sure don't know," I snap back, trying to push down my own memories. I turn to Stephen. "Do you know?"

"I have no idea but I want to find out so that I can be as good a friend to Anthony as he is to all of us." Stephen wipes off the counter. "There's no way we're going to understand Anthony right now. It's going to take time."

"That's true," Eli says. "And speaking of time, I want to get back to work at my place."

"Me, too." I'm relieved to talk about anything but people who are troubled and lost.

"Thanks for lunch," A devilish grin spreads across Eli's face. "*Father*."

Stephen shakes his head and he laughs. "Get out of here you two."

Chapter 5

As I walk with Eli back to his apartment to finish going through his things, we see S & M coming out of the laundry room with several baskets of Eli's clothes—now fresh and clean and nicely folded.

"S & M, give those to me. We need to store Eli's clothes at my apartment until the professional cleanup crew finishes at his place." I turn to him. "Do you know when they are arriving?"

"Mr. Lake said they're coming tomorrow morning."

"So is it okay with you to keep your clothes at my place for now?"

"It's more than okay." He smiles and I feel my heart melt. "I can't imagine how I would have gotten through any of this without you, Jackson."

"That settles it then." I take the basket from Sarah.

"There's more, boys," Sarah tell us. "Two more baskets and lots of clothes on hangers."

"And don't forget Eli's sheets and towels, S." Martha hands over her basket to Eli.

"We'll bring everything to my place," I tell them. "I can worry about where to put them later."

"Really?" S & M ask in unison with a look of surprise on their faces.

"Yes. Really." I grin, knowing they're wondering why my OCD isn't taking control of me. Truthfully, I'm not sure myself, but Eli needs me. No matter my compulsion I won't let him down.

Martha kisses me on the cheek. "Jackson, leave your door unlocked and we'll bring the rest of Eli's things."

"Oh no you're not," Eli says. "You've done enough for me already. I'll take care of the rest."

She puts her hands on her hips. "Young man, S and I may be old but we're still very capable. We're not dead, you know."

"Now you've gone and done it, Mr. Fireman." I laugh. "How are you going to put out this blaze?"

He shakes his head. "I'm not sure I can."

Just then, we see Harvey coming out of the laundry room with an oversized cart with the rest of Eli's clothes.

Harvey walks up to us. "Hello, ladies. Gentlemen. I thought you might need some assistance with this chore. Are these going to Jackson's for now?"

Eli nods. "Good old Harvey. What would we do without you?"

"Eli was about to get into very hot water with S & M and you saved the day," I say. "Thanks, ladies, for your help."

"What?" Martha shakes her head. "You think S and I aren't helping? You're wrong."

Eli laughs. "Now who is in hot water?"

"Both of you, that's who, especially if you keep trying to make us feel like we're ancient and helpless," Sarah states firmly.

"We would never do that." Eli turns to me. "Right?"

"Right. You two are the most vibrant women I know."

Sarah winks. "Go ahead and carry the clothes inside but M and I are putting them away, understand?"

Eli and Harvey turn to me, obviously waiting for my approval.

Any other place in the world, S & M's actions would seem pushy and intrusive. But not here. Not at Mockingbird Place. Here they are adored, and we all know their actions always come from their loving hearts.

"I have no problem with that. Since Trace has moved out there's plenty of room for his things. The closet is empty. The dresser is empty." I give both wonderful women a hug. "And I know you two very well. When you have made up your mind to help, no one is going to stop you."

"Now you're talking," they say in unison.

We all laugh.

Martha points at my door. "Lead the way, boys."

Once inside my spare bedroom, where Eli is staying, I say to S & M, "We'll place the towels and linens and the basket of under-wear on the bed. We'll also place the hang-up clothes there as well. That way you can organize the pants, shirts, and so on as you go."

Sarah looks at me sternly. "Jackson, I believe M and I can handle this. You know this isn't our first time around a closet or dresser."

"Oh, Sarah, I'm sorry. It's just my OCD kicking in."

"Don't give me any excuses, young man," she says with a grin. "Just lay the clothes on the bed and M and I will take care of everything."

"I should help at least." Eli looks at the clock on the nightstand.

"I saw that," Sarah says. "It's obvious you want to get a little more done at your place before that cleaning crew shows up. We can handle this just fine."

Feeling a little bad about being so bossy, I give her and Martha kisses on the cheek. "Sorry. I love you both so much."

They wrap their arms around me. "We love you, too."

Martha steps back. "Now scat. All three of you."

Eli, Harvey, and I salute her and head downstairs.

At the bottom of the stairs, Eli turns to me. "A couple more hours and we should be finished with all we can do."

"I'd like to pitch in too," Harvey says. "If you don't mind."

"Mind?" Eli puts his arm around the sweet man's shoulders. "We could use your expertise, Harvey. Come on."

We get right to work inside Eli's unit.

As I roll up the last of Eli's ruined rugs, Harvey looks at me.

"Are we still on for Saturday after your tennis match? Meet at your mom's place at seven?""

"Yes." I've been putting off dealing with mom's house for too long. She's been gone almost a year now. *Time to put the past to rest, Jackson.*

"Excellent. I'll bring my tools."

"Not necessary. Just a pen and paper to give me an estimate is all you need." I feel my gut tighten. There are so many bad memories at that house. "You know, Harvey, my match might last longer than expected. Not sure when we'll actually get started. Could we reschedule?"

"Of course we can. We'll keep rescheduling as long as you need to, Jackson." Harvey has a way about him that puts me and everyone else at ease. There's not an ounce of judgment in him. Only acceptance, kindness, and wisdom. "I know this has to be very difficult for you."

"Maybe a year isn't long enough. I'm not sure I'm ready to deal with mom's house just yet."

"I can't imagine what you're going through," Eli says to me. "If I ever lost my mother I don't know what I would do."

He's got to be the most compassionate fireman in the department, but he doesn't know the whole story about my mom. No one at Mockingbird Place does except Trace.

"Harvey, let's keep the appointment. I can do this." *I have to do this.*

"You got it, buddy." Harvey places his hand on my shoulder. "Leave it to me. We'll get your mom's house back in order."

Will he feel the same way once he sees how bad it is? At least it's been cleaned out thanks to the crew Aunt Jenny and I hired. Harvey won't have to deal with mom's stuff, but he will have to face the disaster and shambles that is left.

"Shall we get back to it, guys," I say, hoping the work will occupy all of my mind and keep me from time traveling back into the past.

"Absolutely." Eli's big blue eyes are the perfect distraction for me.

When the last of the tasks are done, I turn to Harvey. "That went much faster than I thought, thanks to you."

"That's for sure," Eli says. "Thank you so much."

"My pleasure. I've got your new windows ordered. I'll get them installed as soon as they arrive."

"How about I buy you and Jackson dinner tonight to show my appreciation?" Eli asks.

"Not necessary." Harvey puts his tape measure back into his toolbox. "I'd love to join you two but I can't tonight. Believe it or not, this old man has a date."

I'm so excited for him. "Oh my God, Harvey. That's great."

"It sure is," Eli says. "How about a rain check, Harvey? That way Jackson and I could double date with you and your new boyfriend."

Double date? As much as I wish it could be a double date, Eli and I can only be friends.

"You're jumping the gun, Eli Grayson." Harvey grins. "I never said he's a boyfriend." Then he winks at us. "At least not yet. That remains to be seen. This is only our first date, fellas."

I can tell that Harvey is really looking forward to his evening with his date. "One thing's for sure, you're handsome and charming enough. I just hope this mystery man of yours is handsome and charming enough for you."

Harvey nods. "One thing for sure, Nathan is very handsome in his profile picture on the site. And you should hear his sexy voice on the phone. We've been talking for a couple of weeks now. I'm actually quite nervous about meeting him in person. I haven't been on a date in years—and that was with my wife, God rest her soul."

"Don't worry, Harvey," Eli says. "It will be fun. Trust me."

"Okay. I'll take your word for it. And now I better hurry home so I can get cleaned up and ready to go. I want to look my best." Harvey smiles. "Wish me luck, fellas."

"You got it, my friend." After he leaves, I turn to Eli. "If anyone deserves happiness it's Harvey."

"That's the truth. I'm already anxious to find out what happens on his date, but we'll have to wait until tomorrow to get the details."

Eli scans the apartment. "We've done all we can for now. The cleaning crew will be here first thing in the morning."

"How about we go get a shower at my place and then finish off the day with a warm meal and a movie?"

"Jackson, I'm really too tired to cook. How does Chinese delivery sound to you?"

"You must have been reading my mind because I was just thinking how tired my body feels. It would be nice just to relax and eat at home. I have a brand new bottle of wine that would go perfect with Chinese food."

"That sounds good." He kisses me on the cheek, causing a fiery spark inside me. "Shall we go?"

"Yes. Let's." Every time I feel like I've gotten control of my feelings for Eli he goes and does something like kissing me on the cheek, which sends me into another tailspin of confusion. If Scott wasn't in the picture I would be thrilled to let my feelings out and see where they take me…take us. Am I being ridiculous? Eli sent Scott away today. Maybe he has things more under control concerning his ex than I thought.

Forty-five minutes later, I step out of my shower and grab a towel from one of the racks. I can't help but smile, seeing how neatly Eli folded his towel on the other rack. I wonder if he did that just for me, or could he be a little OCD as well? Either way, it pleases me.

I can't get the image of him coming out of the bathroom earlier —*freshly showered and wearing only pajama bottoms*. Mm. That man is off-the-charts sexy. I can hear him downstairs ordering food from my favorite Chinese restaurant.

I bring my fingers up to the spot on my cheek he kissed. He's got everything I find attractive in a man. Good looks. Warm personality. Honesty. Kindness. The whole package. Could there be a chance for us? I'm beginning to think there might be. There's no sense in closing the door so tightly. Or is there?

Damn it. Why am I being so hot and cold?

"What harm would it be to just try?" I look at my six-pack in the mirror. "Jackson McAllen, pajama bottoms it is."

I quickly finish getting cleaned up, putting on my pajama bottoms. Leaving the bathroom as neat as I found it, I walk to my bedroom and put my folded pajama top in the dresser. Excited at the possibility for another kiss from the super-hot fireman, I take a deep breath and walk down the stairs.

Chapter 6

O nce downstairs, I see Eli is talking on his phone. "I understand but you need to calm down. It's going to be okay."

Shit. It's not the Chinese restaurant he's giving our order to. I can tell by the sound of Eli's strained tone that Scott is the one on the other end of the call.

"Scott, just take a deep breath and I will be there in ten minutes."

Damn it, I was right. I should have known this was too good to be true.

"I'll hurry. I promise." Eli clicks off his phone. "Jackson, I'm so sorry but—"

"Nothing to be sorry about," I say in the most nonchalant tone I can muster. "You need to go I assume."

He nods. "No time to tell you about what's going on right now but I will fill you in later."

"I have a pretty good idea what's going on, Eli, or better yet *who.*"

"I promise it's not what you think."

"Really? Scott isn't trying to manipulate you once again?" I can tell by the look on his face that my words hurt him.

"Maybe so, but Jackson, there is more to this than you can imagine. Sorry, but I've got to hurry and change and get to him. Can we just please sit down and talk when I come back and I'll explain everything?"

"Sure, buddy. Whatever. I'm not going anywhere tonight. I'll be here. But I do have my tennis match tomorrow, so I won't be up all night."

"Okay. I'll hurry as fast as I can."

I watch Eli run up the stairs.

Less than a minute later, he's out the door leaving me alone in my apartment.

"Damn it, Jackson. Stop feeling sorry for yourself. You and Eli are just friends."

Seeing Eli has already opened the bottle of wine, I pour myself a glass. Vibrating with frustration, I take a sip and notice my coffee table needs a good dusting. Right now you could write your name on it. How could I have let that happen? Have I been so wrapped up in Eli that I haven't noticed it? I get my dusting cloth and polish and run it across the surface of the table. When I look at the cloth I realize that not a single spec of dust is on it. The table was perfectly clean the whole time.

"What's the matter with me?" I ask myself, but I already know the answer. Whenever I'm anxious or frustrated or angry or whatever emotion I can't quite deal with I go into a whirlwind of cleaning. That has always been my way to handle things. No matter what it is. Why? Probably because of the way I grew up. *With my mom. In her house.*

I swore that would never happen to me. But what do I do? Just the opposite. I'm a fucking cleaning freak.

Not caring if things need dusting or not, I run the cloth over the rest of the surfaces in my apartment—the bookshelf, the side tables, the counter. Everywhere. When I finish, I feel more in control of myself, but that doesn't mean I'm not upset that Eli left and went to Scott.

The doorbell rings. That's got to be mine and Eli's dinner.

Still in my pajama bottoms I open the door and find not just the guy delivering the Chinese food but also Brad Duncan, who is on the university tennis team with me.

"Hi, Jackson." Brad grins, pulling out his wallet. "Let me get your dinner. It's on me."

"That's not necessary, Brad."

"But it is. It's the least I can do for dropping in on you without calling first." He turns to the delivery guy, handing him a one-hundred-dollar bill. "Will that cover it?"

"That more than covers it including the tip, but I don't have enough change to give you."

"Keep it." Brad takes the food from him.

Staring at Benjamin Franklin, the guy's eyes widen. He looks up and says, "Thanks." Then he rushes away, clearly thrilled at his incredible good fortune this evening.

He is lucky. I would have only been able to tip him five bucks.

I'm not surprised at Brad's excessive generosity. I've seen it before on many occasions. Brad comes from a very wealthy family and is quite free with gifts and picking up checks. Some of our teammates think he's a show-off, but I think he uses his bank account to overcompensate his insecurity.

"Sorry to show up so late, Jackson, but I just learned about the fire at your neighbor's house. That's why I'm here. To make sure you're okay."

"I'm okay. But you and I should be sleeping. We've got our doubles match tomorrow."

"We're fine, Jackson. You know we're going to win. We always do."

"I'm glad you're so confident, but don't get cocky."

"I'll try." Brad holds up the sacks of Chinese food. "You've got enough here to feed five people." He laughs and then looks me straight in the eyes. "Mind if I join you?" Typical Brad. Pay to get his way, which puts me in an awkward position, feeling I must invite him in, though I'm not really in the mood for company right now.

So of course I say, "Come on in, Brad." I lead him to the kitchen and get out two plates for us. I glance at the open bottle of wine and my glass, which is still full. But the wine is for Eli and me, not Brad. I want to enjoy it while we have that discussion Eli promised once he gets back. So I get the pitcher of tea out of the refrigerator and pour us each a glass. "I'm going to put on a shirt."

He grins. "You look just fine to me."

"Thanks, but I'm not comfortable. I'll be right back, Brad." As I walk up the stairs to my bedroom, I remember Trace saying he knew Brad was interested in me. At the time I didn't think so, since Brad was in a relationship with Cathy, a freshman cheerleader. But Brad broke it off with Cathy over a month ago and came out to the team and me. Ever since he's been showing up at my place, even though I've made it very clear that we can only be friends. He just won't give up.

I put on my pajama top and head back downstairs.

Brad is dishing out the food on our plates, which frustrates me, especially since he's spilled rice all over my counter. He's making himself at home like he's my boyfriend.

He looks at me. "Forks or chopsticks?"

As I clean up the mess he's made, I say firmly, "Just sit down, Brad. I'll take care of this for us."

"Okay. Sorry." He steps back. "I forgot about your OCD. You're in charge, not me."

"That has nothing to do with it." I realize my words are coming out harsher than I intend. So I try to soften my tone. "I'm just not comfortable with other people in my kitchen."

"I get it. No worries, Jackson."

I smile, hoping to put him at ease. "How about you? Fork or chopsticks?"

"Chopsticks will work fine for me."

"My roommate will be coming back so I would like to save some for him." Wondering when Eli will return from Scott's place, I feel my gut tighten. This night isn't going the way I would like. Not one damn bit.

"Roommate?" Brad looks surprised and a bit irritated. "Did that guy Trace move back in with you?"

"No, he hasn't. Still living in Unit E with Luke and Ava and the baby."

"That's good to hear. I wasn't sure things would last with him and his cowboy," he says with a hint of sarcasm in his voice.

Trace and Brad are like oil and water. They don't care for each other and they certainly don't mix.

"I have absolutely no doubt that Trace and Luke will be together forever. Now, let's eat. I'm starving."

"Me, too. But you haven't answered my question. Who's your new roommate?"

"Eli. His place burned and I offered him my spare bedroom until he can move back into his apartment."

"The fireman? That was his place? Unit C?"

"That's him."

"That guy is a prick." He frowns. "I've only been around him a couple of times but it's obvious to me he's got the hots for you. I saw how he looked at you at Trace's art show. And he was glued to you at the last barbeque around the pool."

I'm a little shocked by Brad's attitude. "Even if Eli does have the hots for me, why would that make him a prick?"

"You should just stay away from him."

"Eli is a good guy, Brad."

"Doesn't he have a boyfriend?"

"Ex-boyfriend," I answer, wondering if Eli is still with Scott.

Brad sighs. "I know I'm out of line, but I don't trust that fireman."

"If you got to know him better I'm sure you would change your mind." But do *I* really trust Eli? Eli is always running to Scott's side after all.

"Jackson, there's no way I would ever change my mind about Eli Grayson."

"I didn't know you knew his last name."

"I think you mentioned it to me a couple of times. Or maybe it was one of your neighbors who told me at one of the parties here. I don't remember." He shrugs. "I'm sorry. I just don't want you to get hurt."

"That's okay. How about we forget about it and enjoy this food you bought?"

"Perfect."

We sit at the table and start chatting about the team, our new coach, the upcoming match, and all sorts of interesting things. Brad and I have a lot in common. We both love playing tennis, Chinese food, B-rated movies, photography, and being outdoors. I find myself really enjoying his company.

"Wow. I'm full." He pushes his plate to the side. "It was so good."

I take one last bite before clearing the table. "Yes, it was. Thank you for buying."

"My pleasure, but Jackson, there's something else I'd like to give you. I would love to take you to Banff National Park in the Canadian Rockies. The hiking there is out of this world."

"I've heard it is. That would be a great trip, but I don't have the funds for it. You know. Poor college student."

"But that's just it. It would be my treat. Mom and Dad have a cabin near the park. I've been going there every summer as long as I can remember. The lodging would be free and all we would need is plane tickets to get there."

"And food."

"The pantry is always full. The caretakers make sure of that. Please say yes, Jackson. It would be so amazing."

"It does sound like it would be fun." Caught up in Brad's enthusiasm, I say, "Maybe we can go but only if I pay for my flight."

"You got a deal." He gives me a hug. "You made my day."

Am I making a mistake with Brad? Pushing him away? Most guys would be thrilled to have him as their boyfriend. Unlike Eli, he doesn't come with any baggage.

Brad brings out his phone. "I'll order our tickets right now."

"Wait a second. I said 'maybe.' I haven't made up my mind yet."

"But I have made up my mind for us. Just leave everything to me. I promise you won't regret it."

I realize I've been right all along about Brad. He and I would never work out. He's too...too pushy. And always trying to take control.

Hoping to give myself time to think about his offer, I say, "I may end up taking some classes this summer, so it might not be possible for me to go."

He frowns. "You're just saying that because I'm bisexual and not one hundred percent gay, right?"

I sigh. "No, Brad. That's not it."

"Have you ever dated a bisexual guy before?"

"No. I can honestly say I haven't, but that doesn't have—"

"Let me put your mind at ease. For me, when I'm in a relationship all my focus is on that person. That one person meets all my needs, and hopefully, I meet their needs too." He puts his hands on my shoulder. "You know what I mean?"

I step back. "Of course I do, but you're rushing things. We're just friends. Teammates. We're not dating."

"Not yet, but that could change. I could change your mind, Jackson."

"I don't think so."

"Just give me a chance. You'll see I'm right. We're perfect for each other." He grabs me and plants a big kiss on my lips.

I hear my front door open.

Chapter 7

I push Brad back and see Eli standing in the doorway with a shocked look on his face.

"Jackson, I didn't mean to interrupt," he says. "Sorry." Without another word, he walks up the stairs.

Damn it. This night is turning out to be a total fucked-up mess.

Brad glares at me. "I thought you called him a roommate. It seems much more than that to me."

"I really don't care what you think, Brad. I just need you to go."

"Jackson, I'm sorry about the kiss. Is that what's wrong?"

"There's a lot wrong, Brad. Not just with the kiss but with everything. You and I are never going to be more than friends. You need to understand that. I'm sure there's someone out there for you but it's not me." Everything inside me wants to get upstairs to Eli and make it clear to him that what he saw wasn't real. "Please just go."

"Okay, I'll go, but we have more to talk about."

"No. We don't have any more to say." Being anxious, I grab his arm and lead him to the door. "Goodnight, Brad."

He steps out of my apartment and turns back to me. "You're making a big mistake, Jackson. A very big mistake."

I recall Eli's ex saying the same thing. "You're the second person today to tell me that, but it's my decision. Good-bye, Brad. I'll see you at the match tomorrow afternoon." I shut the door.

Without hesitating, I run upstairs and knock on Eli's bedroom door.

No answer.

"Eli, please. Let me in."

The door opens slowly.

"What do you want, Jackson?" he asks sharply.

"I thought we were going to talk."

"That's what I thought too, and I come home and find you in the arms of some guy. You didn't trust my judgment about checking on Scott, did you?"

"Actually, Eli, I didn't. I've seen how he manipulates you."

"That's your perception. You still don't know the whole story."

"Then what is the whole story? I'm all ears." I take a deep breath, realizing I'm being an ass. "Let's calm down."

"Honestly, it's hard to calm down after what I saw, Jackson."

Is he jealous of me and Brad? Or is he talking about something that happened at Scott's condo?

"Eli, can we go downstairs and talk this over the way we planned to in the first place. That bottle of wine is waiting on us."

The tightness in his face relaxes a little. "Okay. I could definitely use a glass of wine right now."

Once downstairs and with wine in hand, we sit next to each other on the sofa.

Breaking the silence at the exact same time, we say in unison, "You go first. No you."

We both smile and our moods lighten a bit.

"You first," I tell him. "I'm anxious to hear about Scott."

"When I was on the phone with Scott, he was out of control and in a very dark place. Scott told me that he couldn't take it anymore and was thinking about killing himself."

"Like I told you before, Eli. He was manipulating you. You don't actually think he would kill himself, do you?" The second the question leaves my mouth I know I'm acting like a jealous lover, not a student aspiring to be a psychologist one day.

"You really don't understand, Jackson. Scott is bipolar and suffers with severe depression. He's attempted suicide several times."

"I didn't know." I feel guiltier than ever about what I said. Still, learning that Scott has mental issues makes me wonder again if he could be the one who started the fire in Eli's unit.

"There's a stigma surrounding mental illness. I guess that's why I've never told you or any of our other neighbors about Scott's issues."

My mind immediately brings up an image of my mother, but I shake it off as quickly as I can. It's too painful.

"Eli, mental illness is just that—an illness like cancer, high blood pressure, or diabetes." I say it firmly, as if I truly believe it myself. But I remember how ashamed I was of my mother and her house. I've only told a few people the real cause of her death.

"Jackson, you have a better understanding about mental illness than I ever imagined." He takes another sip of wine. "When Scott and Kevin lost their parents to a drunk driver, Scott spiraled out of control. Kevin, being the older brother, did what he could, but Scott needed professional help. When the doctors were able to get Scott through it, Kevin was elated. Soon after, he introduced me to Scott, who through counseling and medication was in a very good place at the time." Eli's eyes lock with mine. "Jackson, you may find this hard to believe but Scott is a great guy once you get to know him."

"Maybe so."

"I realized right away that he could only be like a brother to me, not a lover. The first time I tried to get him to understand that was one of the worst days in both our lives. I met him for coffee. Scott was a wreck, but I felt like I'd finally gotten through to him. I went on duty right after. I was going to let Kevin know what happened but we were called out to a four-alarm fire. Kevin died that very same day." With his eyes welling up with tears, Eli stares at his glass, but I know he's not seeing the wine. Instead, I'm certain he's reliving that horrible moment in the past.

I grab his hand to let him know I'm listening, but I remain silent.

"Kevin was my best friend. Before he died in my arms he made me promise to take care of Scott. That's why I moved Scott into my place. I thought that I could help him from slipping back into severe depression. He took it to mean we were going to be together forever. I know now that I fucked up. Whenever I tried to explain things to him he would lash out and hit me. Life with him was so volatile. I've lost it with Scott on more occasions than I care to remember, even though I know I shouldn't. It's just so hard with him, but I have to honor my word to Kevin."

"And you have, Eli, but you still deserve a life of your own."

"But a promise is a promise. Besides, I care a lot for Scott. I'm not going to abandon him when he's in a dark hole that he can't find his way out of on his own."

"You may not believe me, but I do understand. I understand more than you know." I refill our glasses. "Where is Scott?"

"He voluntarily went to the hospital for observation, thank God. I need the time to clear my head and get some rest."

I can relate to how Eli is feeling. I felt the same exhaustion and helplessness when I was dealing with my mom. "Does his doctor realize that Scott's in love with you but you're not in love with him? Couldn't that be an issue for him and his state of mind?"

"I really don't know. I never thought about it, but it would explain some of his harsh reactions to me."

"It's just something you and his doctor might need to discuss."

He nods. "I would never do anything to hurt him. I'm meeting with his doctor in the morning and I'll let her know."

I understand Eli's compassion for Scott and realize that he's not responding to his ex's manipulation. Eli stays in Scott's life because he has such a big heart and genuinely wants to help him.

"Jackson, you certainly know a lot about mental disease."

This would be the perfect opportunity to tell him about my mother, but I'm not ready. "My major is psychology."

"I didn't know that. Are you planning on being a psychologist?"

"I have been considering it, but the amount of schooling is a bit overwhelming. Not sure what I'm going to do after I have my bachelor's degree."

"In my opinion, you would make a wonderful psychologist."

I smile, though I'm not as sure as Eli about me being able to help people who suffer with mental issues. I certainly couldn't help my mom.

Eli finishes his glass of wine. "I'm getting a buzz."

"From just two glasses?"

"Two *big* glasses that you keep refilling." He smiles and holds his glass up to me.

"Empty stomachs and wine can be a dangerous combination, but if you insist." I pour the last of the wine in his glass.

"If I didn't know better, Jackson, I would think you were trying to get me drunk so you could take advantage of me."

"You found me out, Eli. So instead, I'll get you a plate of Chinese food." I walk into the kitchen.

"Tell me who that guy was that you were lip-locking with when I walked in."

"It wasn't a lip-lock, Eli. It was a lip rape, if you must know. Brad is a guy on the tennis team who won't take a hint."

"Got the hots for you, does he? Can't blame him. You're a gorgeous, charming, and wonderful man."

I smile. "I think the wine is going to your head faster than I realized. Here." I hand him a plate of food. "This should help. I'll see if you say the same things about me after you're sober."

"I may not say it, Jackson. You know the old saying about wine being a truth serum. Still, I won't stop thinking it. Hell, I've been thinking it for quite some time."

Everything inside is yelling for me to kiss him. But Eli has so much baggage. He's dealing with Scott's issues. That's got to consume whatever little time he has left over after he finishes his job as a fireman. How can there be any chance for us?

Eli takes a bite of the Chinese food. "This is delicious."

"Told you. You want some more wine?" I hold up the bottle.

"That would defeat the purpose of sobering me up." His wicked grin gives me the trembles.

No man has ever given me the trembles before.

"Just a glass of water, if you don't mind, Jackson." Eli eats another forkful.

"You got it." I hand him the water and sit down next to him.

Eli puts his hand on my leg and squeezes. "You're quite the host."

These aren't trembles I'm feeling now. This is a total earthquake.

I turn my head to look at him but before I can say anything, Eli presses his lips to mine. He deepens his kiss, grabbing me by the back of my neck with one hand and touching the side of my face with the other. I feel my entire being respond. I shouldn't but I can't help myself.

Holding me tight, he asks, "Now do you believe me that it wasn't the wine?"

"Yes, I believe you. But what are we getting ourselves into, Eli?"

"Something wonderful." He kisses me again and the earthquake shakes me to my core. "I've been wanting to kiss you for the longest time. God, your lips are even sweeter than I ever imagined."

More kisses. More trembles. More earthquakes. Want and heat rise up in me, driving me wild. I want him. I want him more than anything.

I'm in a trap but I don't want to get out, God help me. He's just so...so...everything I ever dreamed of. I gaze into his gorgeous blue eyes and imagine what it would be like to stay in his arms, like this, for the rest of my life.

Tenderly, his lips wander over my neck as he unbuttons my shirt. I feel his hands on my bare skin and a shiver rolls through me, washing away logic and hesitation. Nothing will stop me from what I want, what I need. I pull his T-shirt off and stare at his perfectly ripped torso.

When he moves his hands down my sides, I wrap my arms around him, surrendering everything—doubts and worries—to the immense hunger and undying thirst I have for him. A hunger and thirst that will only be satisfied devouring and tasting him.

His phone starts buzzing, and I feel my body tense. "Don't answer it, Eli."

He kisses me lightly on the lips. "I'm sorry but I must. It could be Scott or the hospital."

Letting go of me, he reaches for his phone.

"Hello." Eli looks at me. "I understand. Yes, doctor. I can be there in ten minutes."

In that moment, I come to my senses. This won't ever work. Not with Scott still in the picture. And it's very clear that Scott is *always* going to be in the picture.

Eli clicks off his phone. "Jackson, I'm so sorry."

"Don't be," I say sharply. "I get it. Scott needs you." I stand and start clearing the dishes.

"I hate this but please try to understand. Scott's doctor has given him medication but it's not working. Scott is still screaming my name. His doctor wants to see if I can get him to calm down. If I don't go they're going to restrain him."

I watch him put his T-shirt back on. He walks over and leans in to give me a kiss.

I step back. "You better hurry."

"Jackson, I wish I didn't have to go." The conflict in his eyes is easy to see, but it doesn't change how frustrated I feel. "You have to believe me."

"Just go, Eli. Go to him."

He sighs and walks out the door.

Through the window, I watch him hurrying down the sidewalk to the parking lot. Despite Scott's situation putting a wedge between Eli and me, my aggravation softens a bit.

I realize what a complete jerk I'm being. He told me why he feels so responsible for Scott. Why am I acting like this? I want to run out the door to catch Eli before he drives away to tell him I'm the one who needs to apologize. But my feet feel frozen and I can't seem to move an inch. What's holding me in place? Even though I understand how Eli feels, I know Scott will always come between us.

Swirling with emotion, I grab the broom and begin sweeping.

Chapter 8

Everything inside my unit is dusted, mopped, straightened, and put away. But my *insides* are still reeling. I should be in bed. I'm going to suck tomorrow on the court. But I just can't sleep. Not now. Not with my mind swirling.

I told Eli that I understood why he felt responsible for Scott. I meant it. But do I really understand? Is that why I'm acting this way?

I look at the time on my cell. Almost midnight. Eli hasn't come back yet.

Realizing I don't have any answers, I grab the trash can and march out the door to the dumpster.

Snow comes up, purring.

"You need a little love, sweetie." I reach down and pet her. She stays. "At least you don't run away from me."

She follows me to the dumpster.

As I toss the garbage, I see a car pull into the parking lot. Eli? But when I recognize Trace's car, I know Eli still must be at the hospital. *With Scott.*

As the white cat wanders away, Trace waves at me. "You mind giving me a hand?"

"With what?" I walk over to him.

"Little Mick's diaper bag. The little guy woke up and wouldn't go back to sleep. I didn't want to disturb Luke or Ava. Ava has been cramming for a test she has on Monday and Luke needs his rest for the rodeo." He opens the back door, pulls out the diaper bag, and hands it to me. "You and Eli are coming to see Luke compete, aren't you?"

I'm looking forward to going to my first gay rodeo. "Everyone is coming, Trace."

He smiles and retrieves the baby, who is sound asleep in the carrier. "A car ride works like magic for my sweet boy."

"By the way he looks right now, it certainly seems so."

"Emptying trash after midnight?" His eyes narrow. "What's wrong, Jackson?"

"You can read me better than anyone." I sigh. "A lot is wrong."

"Let's get little Mick back in his crib and I'll put on a pot of coffee. It's been a long time since we had a late night heart to heart. How does that sound?"

Even though I should be in bed for tomorrow's match, I say, "Trace, that sounds perfect." I set my empty trash can inside my patio and follow him to his place.

We walk into the backdoor of Unit E. Trace has been living here with Luke, Ava, and the baby for a few months now. The apartment is warm and inviting. The walls are covered with Trace's paintings. He is so talented and I'm glad he's able to show his work without reservation. The change in him is because of *his* cowboy, Luke, who he just married. Both their parents are thrilled. We all are.

"I'll be right back," Trace says. "If you want you can start the coffee."

I nod, and he quietly heads upstairs with little Mick.

God, I miss having Trace across the hall at my place, but I wouldn't have it any other way. He's deliriously happy.

Opening the cabinet, I'm impressed how organized things are—all the labels facing out and alphabetized. It looks exactly like my cabinets. This is Trace's handiwork. Living with me clearly had an impact on him. I grin. Not that that's always a good thing.

When the coffee is nearly finished, Trace comes back into the kitchen. "Sorry I took so long. I had to sing a couple of verses of 'Twinkle, Twinkle Little Star' just to be sure little Mick stayed asleep when I put him down."

"Perfect timing. It just finished brewing."

Trace pulls out a couple of mugs and fills them. "Let's sit at the table and you tell me what's going on."

I nod and take a seat. Trying to figure out how to start the conversation, I lift the mug to my mouth and drink the coffee. "Mm. This is very good."

Trace grins. "You would say that. You made it. Now what's wrong between you and Eli?"

"You never do beat around the bush, do you?"

"I'm here to help you, buddy, just like you helped me. Now talk."

"I'm an asshole, Trace. A giant fucking asshole. And I'm also an idiot."

"Uh, you may be a little OCD, but I've never ever seen you be an asshole before, much less an idiot."

"Well, I was tonight. I kissed Eli and then I acted like a jerk."

"This sounds more serious than I thought."

We finish the entire pot of coffee as I tell him everything that happened between Eli and me.

"So you see, Trace. I was an asshole. I was an idiot."

"So you're human. We all make mistakes. A very normal reaction. I understand why you feel like you're in second place with Eli, but it's not true. I've seen how Eli looks at you, especially these last couple of days since the fire. It's obvious he cares deeply for you, but it's up to you to be patient with him until he gets through these problems with Scott. And he will get through them. You should know better than anyone how difficult it is to deal with mental illness."

"That's just it. I do understand. There is no end to it. Scott is always going to be a part of Eli's life. I see that now, and I understand why."

Trace leans forward in his chair. "Eli told you that he doesn't think of Scott as a boyfriend."

"But he still cares for Scott. I can't ask him to walk away from the guy. Scott is in trouble and needs Eli." I look down at my empty cup. "Eli would never forgive himself if he walked away and something horrible happened to Scott. Believe me, I know."

Trace grabs my hand. "When are you going to stop blaming yourself, Jackson? You didn't walk away from your mother."

"Yes, I did. I moved out. I abandoned her."

"You were only sixteen, Jackson. You didn't abandon her. You abandoned her stuff. You were always there for her. I know the whole story. The state told your mom that she must clean up the house or they would remove you. Your mom made her choice. That's when you went to live with your Aunt Jenny and met Malcolm, right?"

I nod, remembering the very first day I was introduced to that amazing man. "He knew my Aunt Jenny. She called him the very night CPS forced me to leave. I wouldn't talk to Aunt Jenny. I shut her out. She knew I was gay and since Malcolm was gay, too, she thought I might be more inclined to open up to him about my issues with Mom. She was right. God, I never trusted anyone until I met Malcolm. He always said the right thing."

Trace sighs. "And was always ready to listen when any of us needed someone to talk to."

"I miss him so much. I don't know how I would have survived if he hadn't been there for me. But none of that changes anything, Trace. I could have moved back in with Mom when I turned eighteen. I could have helped her. I might have made a difference. She could still be alive if I had...if I had—"

"Gone back home?" Trace shakes his head. "How many eighteen-year-olds would have known what to do? You and your aunt hired a professional organizer who specializes in people like your mom. That didn't work. You got her to meet with that psychologist who works with those who suffer with hoarding disorders. That didn't work either. The doctors and experts couldn't help your mom. So why do you think you could have? Quit blaming yourself."

"I can't help it, Trace. And now she's gone."

"I wish I could help you with the guilt you're feeling about your mother. I know your aunt worries about that too. Jenny loves you very much."

"I love her too." I close my eyes and take in a deep breath. "And I'm the one who keeps thinking about the baggage Eli has with Scott? Ridiculous. I'm the one with the baggage. I will not fuck up Eli's life too."

"We all have baggage, Jackson. That's what makes us human." Trace lowers his head, which is a clear sign to me that he's struggling with something.

"We've been going on and on about my issues. It's obvious that you've got something on your mind too." Full of concern for my best friend and ready to switch off the topic about Eli and Scott, I ask, "What's up?"

Trace smiles. "Now who's not beating around the bush?"

"We lived together a long time, buddy. I guess I picked up some of your traits over the years."

"Same here, but don't you dare tell anyone I admitted that. And I won't tell on you either."

"We're getting off-track, Trace. What's bothering you?"

"Ava is going on another date with Harrison, you know, the guy in her English class. That's the problem."

"Problem?" I take our cups and the coffeepot to the sink. "Don't you and Luke like him? Hasn't Ava been out with him several times?"

"Yes. Yes, we like him." Trace wipes off the table and joins me in the kitchen, reminding me that we are alike in many ways. "And yes, she's been out with Harrison on lots of dates. That's what scares me. It scares Luke too. What happens if Ava and Harrison fall in love? They'll move in together. Maybe eventually get married."

"And that's a bad thing?"

"No. Yes. Maybe. I know Ava deserves all the happiness in the world. Losing little Mick's father to that drunk driver nearly destroyed her. I want her to be happy. I really do. But even though it's selfish of me, I can't help wondering where that will leave Luke and me if she falls in love with Harrison? On the outside looking in. That's where, Jackson. We can't lose our son. We just can't. I can't live apart from Little Mick and neither can Luke. We don't want to be visiting dads who only get him on the weekend and some holidays. We want to be a part of his life every day."

Hearing the emotion in Trace's every word makes me realize how difficult Ava dating Harrison is for him and Luke. "First of all, Trace, they've only been dating a short time. You're worried about something that may or may not happen. But even if it does, Ava told me that Harrison thinks you and Luke are incredible guys. If things continue to progress for them, who says the four of you can't live together with little Mick?"

"You really think that's a possibility?"

From behind us, I hear Ava say, "It's more than a possibility, Trace. Jackson is right. I would never leave you and Luke out. We're family."

Trace and I turn around to face Ava, who still looks stunning despite having just gotten out of bed.

"On our very first date I told Harrison that we were a package deal. And guess what? He didn't run away. And since then we've discussed it a lot." She moves right in front of Trace. "You and Luke have nothing to worry about. If it's Harrison or someone else I end up with, we will all be together. Little Mick will have three doting dads and one happy mommy. He'll be one of the luckiest little boys in the world."

I see Trace's eyes well up and the weight of worry lifting off of him.

"Oh, Ava." He grabs her and pulls her in for a hug.

"I should have said something to you and Luke, Trace. But I thought you knew that I always wanted you to live with us." She steps back and looks at him straight in the eyes. "That's what I still want. That's never going to change. We're family. You and Luke will always be little Mick's dads."

I hear Luke coming down the stairs.

Holding the baby, he smiles. "Is there room for two more at this party?"

Clearly overwhelmed at what Ava has told him, Trace rushes to Luke's side and gives him a big kiss.

"I'll take that as a yes."

"Oh honey, you won't believe what Ava just told me. We've been worrying for nothing. This is the best news ever. It's all going to be just fine. Better than fine."

I laugh at Trace's overexcitement.

"Slow down, baby," Luke tells him softly.

"But I can't slow down, Luke. It's just too good to keep in." Trace turns to me. "Right, Jackson? It's incredible news."

"Yes it is. Incredible." I chuckle and look at Luke. "I may be to blame. With the excitement and the pot of coffee your husband and I just shared, it may be impossible for him to put on the brakes and be coherent."

Luke shakes his head. "Please, will somebody tell me what you are talking about? What did you tell Trace, Ava?"

"I just didn't know you guys were so worried, Luke, or I would have already told you."

"For crying out loud, told me what? Please. I can't stand this anymore."

Trace kisses him again. "Nothing is going to change. No matter what happens with her and Harrison. Ava wants us to all live together, forever."

Luke's eyes widen. "What?"

Ava wraps her arms around him and Trace. "You silly cowboy. We are family. Get it? Wherever little Mick and I go—you go. You are his dads."

"Should I put on another pot of coffee?" I ask them. "I doubt any of us are going to be able to sleep after this group therapy session."

Ava nods. "Yes, please."

"Group therapy session?" Trace smiles. "That's exactly what this was. And if it hadn't been for Jackson pushing me to let out my feelings we wouldn't have gotten to the answers we needed." He hugs me. "You're going to make a wonderful psychologist one day, buddy."

I shrug. "Who knows?"

"Me. I know."

"Me, too," Ava and Luke say in unison.

I look at the four of them and realize how happy they are and will continue to be.

Even though I'm so glad for them, it also makes me sad knowing that someday they'll be moving away. This apartment can't hold four adults and a child. Too small.

Will I ever be as happy as Trace and his new family are? It's amazing and wonderful to see how far he's come since we first met.

Could there be a chance for me too? For me and Eli? I really wish it could be, but that dark place inside me buried deep under all my baggage is filled with crushing doubt.

Chapter 9

After saying good-bye to Trace, I walk out the backdoor of Unit E and immediately notice Eli's car. My gut tightens. He's back from the hospital. Is he asleep or awake? Noticing all the lights are on at my apartment, I know the answer. He's awake and likely waiting for me to return.

I'm just not ready to face him yet. I still don't have answers. But then again, do I need any answers?

I get a text on my phone.

It's from Eli. *Getting worried. Are we okay?*

I open the gate to my patio, grab the empty trash can, and step up to the back door. Pausing for just a moment and taking a deep breath, I put the keys in the lock and open the door.

Eli is sitting on the sofa in only a pair of shorts. I have to admit the scenery is breathtaking.

"Jackson, thank God you're home. I was worried." He stands and walks over to me.

"Sorry. Just now got your text. I didn't mean to worry you. I was just next door talking with Trace."

Eli hugs me. "The important thing is you're okay."

I step back, and I see the concern in his eyes. "You had to do what you had to do, Eli. What happened with Scott at the hospital?"

"He was completely out of control when I arrived. I don't know if it was me talking with him or him taking the medicine that calmed him down, but either way it worked. I waited until he fell asleep before I came back home."

"Do you know how long they plan on keeping Scott there?"

"I really don't know but I do know he needs long-term help. There's got to be someplace he can go. Someplace where they can help him get through all his misery. I just don't know where that is. Hey, you're a psychology major. Do you know of a treatment center that could help him?"

"There are several, but I'll ask one of my professors which one is the best for Scott."

"Thanks, Jackson. You're the best." Eli stares at me, and I feel a shiver roll up and down my spine. "I'm so sorry I left the way I did."

"It really doesn't matter." I know I'm acting like an ass once again. But how can I help it? I want him. God, I want him. But us being together would end in disaster. A total mess. I can't let that happen. I just can't. So if being an ass will push him away, then that's what I must be. "Goodnight, Eli."

I want to escape, need to escape. Violent and conflicting emotions are tearing my insides apart. I take a single step toward the stairs, but Eli moves in front of me, blocking my exit.

"No, Jackson. This isn't *goodnight*. We are going to talk and work this out." His tone is demanding and forceful. I can imagine it's the same tone he must use when guiding people out of a burning building.

Do I need rescuing? Can he rescue me? Or will my toxic fumes suffocate the life out of him?

"Eli, there's just no room for us with all we have to deal with. You have to get your place put back together. You have to deal with the insurance company. You have to work with the police investigating the fire."

"Hold on, Jackson. Let's back up a bit." He stares at me, and I find it impossible to look away. "What do you mean 'what *we* have to deal with'? "

"I don't know what I meant," I answer. "Besides, there's Scott. What more is there to say, Eli? He needs you. That's the messy fact of things."

"But I need *you*, Jackson." Eli presses his lips to mine and my long list of reasons why we can't be together is erased. "Life is messy, but who cares."

"Now you sound like Trace."

"Trace is right. Listen, Jackson, we can deal with all the things we have to face later. Much later. Right now, it's us. You and me." He kisses me again, and I feel my initial hesitation vanish completely.

I want him. God, I want Eli.

I lean into him, parting my lips slightly, deepening our kiss. Nothing else seems to exist outside our embrace. It's just him and me. Us. Together.

I run my hands over his chiseled body, enjoying the feel of his muscles. Eli removes my shirt and touches me in ways that ignite the fire of desire inside me. Even though I still have doubts, I'm unable to resist him.

"I want you," I confess. "I want all of you."

"Oh, Jackson, I've waited so long to hear you say that." He kisses me again. Slowly, he moves his lips to my neck and whispers in a lusty tone, "And I want you."

Mad with desire, we rip off the rest of each other's clothes.

I've spotted him in the pool before, wearing swimming trunks, but this time, being so close, *so very close*, I get to see every inch of his incredible male physique. And boy, it is very incredible. Rock solid. But it's his blue eyes that mesmerize me.

"Damn, Jackson." He smiles, and I feel like I'm under his spell even more. "I've wanted this for so very long."

"Have you?" I ask in a teasing tone.

He kisses me again. "You know I have."

"I know. I've dreamed about it myself."

"Let me try to make the reality even better than the dream."

Another kiss, deep and lingering, makes me hot all over. Our tongues tangle together.

We're all over each as we make our way to the bedroom. Our passion blazes as we discover each other's bodies with our lips and fingers, wrapping our arms and legs together. I can feel his hard cock pressing against mine, making me want him even more.

He kisses his way from my lips to my neck and down my chest. When he clamps down lightly on my nipples, one with his teeth and the other with his fingers, I let out a groan of sheer pleasure, feeling my need expand inside me.

I run my hands through his hair as he continues licking and pinching my nipples until they're throbbing deliciously, filling me with even more lust for him.

He glances up at me with those big blue eyes of his, and then reaches down, wrapping his hand around my cock. "Better than the dream, Jackson?"

"Oh, yes. Fuck yeah."

He guides me back to the bed, keeping hold of me. "Sit," he orders.

I can't resist him.

Once I'm on the bed, Eli, never letting go of my cock, gets down on his knees between my legs.

"So much better than the dream," I tell him, as my heart races.

Once again that devilish smile of his appears. "And I'm only getting warmed up." He licks the head of my cock, teasing the slit with his tongue.

I lean on my elbows, enjoying the feel of his mouth on me. I don't close my eyes. I want to see him, to let my eyes feast on how he's pleasuring me.

When he swallows me and tenderly squeezes my balls, every nerve in my body engages, hot and electric. Oral sex has never been this intense or this all-consuming before. More pressure builds up inside me. Needing to touch him, I lean forward and grab the back of his head with both hands.

"Oh God, yes, Eli. Yes. So good. So fucking good."

My words seem to have an impact on him, and he swallows even more of me. I see him reach down and begin stroking his hard cock, which drives me even wilder, pushing me closer and closer to a much-needed release.

His mouth is so wet, his lips so tight, his hands so warm.

"Getting close, Eli."

Tightening his hold on me, one hand on my balls and the other stroking his cock, I feel him take more of me into his mouth.

The immense pressure won't be held back much longer. But I want more before it erupts.

"Eli, come join me on the bed. I have to get a taste of you too." I reach down and grab his shoulders to encourage him to get beside me.

When he joins me on the bed, I move into a sixty-nine position.

We both wrap our legs around each other's shoulders, and I kiss his hard cock. It's a beast, pulsing with the beat of his heart. I run my tongue up and down his shaft, feeling him do the same on me. Utterly overwhelmed with the pleasure of being with him, my lust takes over and I swallow his cock until I feel it hit the back of my throat. Our oral strokes synchronize, taking me to a new state of enjoyment I've never experienced with anyone else ever before. It's like we are connected to the very core of each other, and at this very moment there isn't even a single speck of uncertainty inside me. All I want is to pleasure Eli the way he is pleasuring me.

With every matching stroke we give each other, I get closer and closer to the edge of release. Knowing I can't hold back any longer, I try to pull out of his mouth, but he tightens his hold on me, silently letting me know what he wants. I want the same, to taste all he has to offer, to drink every drop of him. We both double our efforts, sucking like two madmen.

At the very moment I feel his cream hit the back of my throat, I orgasm, sending my own cream into his mouth. The powerful climax explodes, vibrating hot pulses throughout my body.

We remain in the sixty-nine position for several necessary breaths.

"Jackson, that was…that was unreal. Incredible."

I flip around so that we are face to face. Smiling, I say, "Much better than the dream."

"Much. Worth the wait." He presses his lips lightly to mine.

It doesn't take long before we start to fall asleep in each other's arms.

I can't explain this feeling I'm having. It's beyond pleasure. It's beyond passion. What is it? It's something I've never experienced before.

Am I falling in love with him?

Chapter 10

I can hear my mother rummaging through papers again. What is so damn important to her this time?

I hate weekends. I'm stuck at home. Nowhere to go. Nowhere to escape.

I look around my bedroom stacked with piles and piles of her useless crap. She promised she would never put anything in my room, but now I can hardly find my bed.

I remember the last time I spent the night away. Kevin had five of us over. What a blast. His mom made us cookies and his dad bought us pizza. I wish I could be like him and my other friends. They get to come home to clean houses with parents who make sure they have food and shelter and their own spaces. They have normal lives. My life is far from normal.

Our house wasn't always like this. Although I was very young when my father died, I remember when he was still around everything was neat and tidy. He and mom even hosted parties for their neighbors and friends. Mom was different back then.

I don't sleep over at any of my friends' now. They would expect to come to my home. No way am I bringing them here to this dirty mess.

I pound my fists on the mattress, which is just as filthy as everything else in this dump. There's so much junk I can't even remove the sheets. And where would

I take them to wash? We have a washer and dryer, but they are stuffed with more of mom's crap. They haven't worked in years. Nothing works. The sinks. The air conditioner. The heater. The stove. The refrigerator. The bathroom. If it weren't for the showers at my school's gym, I would stink like she does.

Looking inside my backpack makes me feel a little better. It's mine. Organized. Clean. Sane.

I hear a crash.

"Jackson, I need you!" The panic in her voice scares me.

I rush through the path between the stacks of junk.

When I get to the kitchen, I find her on the floor with several boxes on top of her. "Mom, don't move." I lift the boxes up and toss them to the side.

"Oh. It hurts, Jackson." Her labored breathing is scaring me.

"I'll get help." Tripping on piles of stuff, I run back to my room to get my phone. As I head back to the kitchen, I dial 9-1-1 and tell the operator our address and what has happened to mom. "Please hurry."

"Stay on the line with me until the EMTs arrive. You'll hear the sirens shortly."

"Yes, ma'am." I kneel down next to my mother. "It's going to be okay, mom. I've got to make sure the ambulance guys can get inside."

"No, Jackson. You can't let them in."

Her words don't surprise me. She doesn't let anyone inside, even Aunt Jenny. Mom is ashamed. She knows she has a problem.

I can hear the sirens getting louder.

Mom groans and closes her eyes.

I squeeze her hand. "It's going to be okay. You're really hurt. They can help you."

I let her go and make my way to the front door.

"Don't leave me, Jackson."

"I'll be right back." I'm not angry with her anymore. I need to be more understanding and not so selfish. She can't help herself. I love her. I want to help her. I will help her.

I hear pounding.

"The ambulance is here," I tell the 9-1-1 operator. "Thank you for your help."

Clicking off the phone, I open the front door as wide as it will go, which is only about ten inches due to the piles next to it. When I come home from school, I always have to squeeze my way in. I see two big men with a stretcher on our porch. One is at least six-one. The other is a couple inches shorter. They're both much larger than me. There's no way that either of them can make it through.

"I'm here. Hold on." Frantically, I start picking up the boxes blocking the door and hurl them as hard as I can into the living room. The door opens another couple of inches.

"Not enough, kid," the taller man says.

"If you'll shove while I pull I think it will work," I tell him.

He nods.

As he leans into the door, I pull with every ounce of strength I have inside me. The rest of the debris gives, and finally the door opens wide.

As they enter, I recognize the shock and disgust on their faces, but I don't care. "My mom is back there."

I lead them on the path to the kitchen.

"Ma'am, we're the EMTs here to help you," the man who leaned against the door tells my mom. "I'm Dave and this is Bill."

Watching them check her, I feel so helpless. So alone. I call Aunt Jenny and tell her what happened.

"Sweetheart, where are they taking your mom?"

"Let me ask them. Sir, what hospital are you going to?"

"Methodist on Colorado," Bill says.

I repeat the information to Aunt Jenny.

She tells me to ask them if I can ride in the ambulance.

"Sirs, my Aunt Jenny would like to know if it would be okay for me to ride to the hospital with my mom?"

"Sure," Dave answers.

"They say I can," I tell her.

"Jackson, I'll meet you there." Aunt Jenny always has my back. She's the one who got me the cell phone. And she's the only one who has tried to help Mom.

I click off the phone just as they place my mom on the stretcher. The groans that come out of her mouth are terrible. "Please don't hurt her."

"We're trying to be as careful as we can, kid," Dave says. "We need your help to go ahead of us and make sure we don't bump into anything."

"Yes, sir."

"Bill, we're going to have to lift the stretcher over our heads, and we'll have to be very careful of the door frames. Kid, you watch for that too, okay?"

"I will, sir."

Bill stares at the piles. "Dave, I'm not even sure that will work with all this stuff in here."

I feel the panic rise up inside me. "It has to work."

"It will." Dave puts his hand on my shoulder.

"Yeah, it will, kid." Bill nods, clearly having a change of heart. "Let's do this."

It takes some effort and time but we are able to get Mom out of the house and into the ambulance.

On the ride to the hospital, I tell her, "I'm with you, Mom. I'm here."

When we arrive, they rush her inside. Aunt Jenny is there to meet us. She runs to me, wrapping her arms around me. Even though I try to hold back the tears, I can't stop them. All the anxiety and fears for my mom come rushing out of me like a flood.

Dave comes over to us a few minutes later. "Kid, your mom is in good hands. She's going to be fine. This must be your Aunt Jenny."

"Yes, I am. Jenny Rogers, Alice's sister."

They shake hands.

"I'm Dave, one of the EMTs who helped take care of Mrs. McAllen. May I have a word with you?"

I remember the look on his and Bill's faces when they came into the house. "You can talk in front of me because I already know what you are going to say."

"Go ahead, Dave," she says. "We're both aware you have to report...this... the condition of my sister's house."

"Yes, ma'am. I do." Dave turns to me. "I'm sorry, kid. But this is my job. You do understand what this means, don't you?"

"Yeah. Sure. I get it. I still want to thank you for helping my mom." I extend my hand, knowing it isn't his fault that we're in this mess.

Dave shakes it. "Thanks for your help, too."

After Dave leaves, Aunt Jenny and I sit down. As we wait for news about Mom, I try to figure out what to do next. Dave is going to file a report about the house. They'll want to take me away. But I can't leave my mom. What can I do? How can I get them to listen to me?

Thirty minutes later the doctor talks to us. "Mrs. McAllen has two broken ribs and a fractured wrist. But what concerns me the most is her breathing. It's probably because of her broken ribs, but I'm going to keep her overnight for observation. If her breathing doesn't improve I want to run some tests in the morning."

"Can I see my mom?" I ask him.

"She was very agitated so we gave her some medicine to calm her down. She needs her rest right now, but you can definitely see her in the morning."

"Thank you, doctor," Aunt Jenny says.

When he walks away, I feel my heart sink. Mom and I are in trouble. Real trouble.

"Jackson, you and I need to talk."

I don't want to talk. I can't. Saying it aloud will make it more real. So I just close my eyes and stay quiet.

"Jackson? Please don't shut me out. I can only imagine how hard this is on you. It's hard on me too. I love your mom. I want her to be okay. You know I've tried. She won't see the psychologist. She won't even let me inside your house anymore. It's worse, isn't it?"

I don't answer. I just can't.

She puts her arm around my shoulder. "You're going to have to come live with me. Maybe then Alice will finally wake up and get the help she needs."

I stand. "I'm the help she needs, Aunt Jenny. If I hadn't been there today when the boxes fell on top of her what would have happened? How long would it have been before someone found her? She could have died. No. I won't leave her. I won't."

Suddenly, the waiting room melts away as the inside of our house comes into focus. I'm standing next to Mom, who is crying as the police try to get me out of the house.

"You have to go, son," she says.

"I won't. I won't leave you." I jerk away from the police officer.

"JACKSON, WAKE UP."

The police officer sounds like Eli.

"You're having a bad dream. Wake up."

I open my eyes and hear myself say, "You can't make me leave."

"I won't even try." Eli looks at me with concern in his eyes.

Realizing I'm back in my bed, I hug him tight. "I'm so relieved. God, I hate reliving that memory."

"Memory? You were asleep."

I lean back on my pillow. "I was, but it's a memory that shows up in my dreams more often than I'd like."

"Do you feel like talking about it?" Eli kisses me on the cheek.

"It's about my mom. I think it's important for you to hear it."

"I'm sorry you lost her, Jackson."

"Thanks. I remember you came to her funeral with everyone else from Mockingbird Place, but what none of you know except Trace is why she died."

He looks surprised. "I thought she had a lung disease."

"That's true, but what's really important to tell you is how she got the disease and how her death could have been prevented."

"It could have been prevented?"

"I think so. It all started when my dad was killed in the line of duty. I was just seven years old. Did I ever tell you my dad was a police officer?"

"No, you didn't. God, Jackson. You've lost both your parents. I can't imagine what you've been through."

"It's tough, but what else can I do but try to get through it? Mom seemed to deal with the pain for a time after dad was killed. Being married to a police officer Mom had always known she might lose him one day. I think what helped her the most was being pregnant with my dad's son, my little brother. She felt like having me and another child would keep my dad's memory alive with her the rest of her life. She even planned on naming the baby after him. But she miscarried a couple of weeks after the funeral and that's when everything really went to hell. Mom wouldn't let any of Dad's things go—silly things, like the last jar of peanut butter he made a sandwich from."

"Maybe not so silly, Jackson. Everyone deals with grief differently."

"I agree, but my mom's behavior continued to become erratic. She didn't stop with just holding on to Dad's stuff but began accumulating more and more things. It started with magazines, newspapers, and grocery bags. She eventually became obsessed with plastic and Styrofoam. It wasn't long before she couldn't part with anything. When I was ten I thought I could make her see what had happened to our home and to her. So, I snuck out several bags to the alley. When Mom discovered what I had done she immediately brought them back into the house. She was furious with me and made me promise never to touch her things again."

When I recount what happened with Mom's accident and how Dave the EMT helped me, he grabs my hand. "God, that's horrible. And you were only fifteen years old. How absolutely awful that was for you."

"After the accident, Mom needed help with her recovery, so she and I went to live with Aunt Jenny. My aunt's house was so perfect, clean and pristine. Aunt Jenny and I were hopeful that she might get better about the hoarding. But as soon as mom was able, she went back home to be with her things. Aunt Jenny tried to convince me to stay with her, but I couldn't leave my mom. Less than a week later, Child Protective Services came to Mom's house. They told her she had one month to clean up the place or I would be removed."

"What happened?"

"She couldn't do it, Eli. Oh, she tried. Mom even tossed that ancient jar of peanut butter into the garbage in the alley, but she had a complete meltdown. I had to go out and retrieve it from the garbage can so she could return to *her normal*. The disease had a hold on her that neither of us could break."

I've never been comfortable sharing this part of my life with anyone. Not even with Trace, who is my best friend. Oh Trace knows, but it wasn't easy to tell him. Why is it so easy to talk to Eli about this? I don't know why, but he seems so understanding.

"What about CPS? Did they come and get you?"

"They came. Because my Aunt Jenny's home was deemed safe they let me live with her. Eli, I didn't have a choice. I was a minor. But when I turned eighteen I could have gone back." The guilt rushes in and threatens to suffocate me. "Maybe that would have been the thing to turn Mom around. But I didn't go back. I just couldn't face the chaos."

"Jackson, you can't blame yourself. Your mom had a disease. That's all. Nothing to be ashamed of. Just a disease. You were not equipped to help her."

"Mom's lungs couldn't take the toxic air in the house. Nothing Aunt Jenny or I said would convince her it was too dangerous to remain there. Her lungs finally gave out. That's what ended her life."

"I'm so sorry, Jackson." He hugs me, and I lean my head on his shoulder. "I'm amazed at how loving you were to your mom. I'm even more amazed that you were able to come out of such heartache to become this incredible man in my arms."

"Incredible? I'm not incredible, Eli. Far from it." How can I not fall in love with him? He's perfect. So perfect. A hero. *And me?* I'm not a hero. And I'm far from perfect. "I'm the one who needs therapy, Eli. I'm damaged goods." When I look into Eli's blue eyes, I feel my heart start to rip inside my chest.

"What's the matter?"

"I'm a jerk. I'm an asshole. I let this go on too long."

"Jackson, what are you saying?"

"You don't need someone like me in your life. I have way too much baggage. *My normal* will make it impossible for us to ever be together. What if something happens and I lose it one day just like Mom did? What then?" Suddenly I feel panic exploding inside me. "Oh God, that would be awful."

"Damn it, Jackson. I don't understand this."

"I hate this. God, I hate this. But what else can I do?"

"You can stop being hot and cold, on and off."

"Damn it, I should have been stronger. I'm not good enough for you. I'm not. I have to end this now before I hurt you." *I. Will. Not. Put my baggage on him.*

I can't bear looking at him. It's just too painful. So instead, I focus my attention on the magazines on my nightstand and start to rearrange them.

Eli comes up behind me and kisses the back of my neck. "You're just afraid. It's okay."

"Stop it, Eli." I jerk free and step away.

He looks stunned.

"*We* are wrong." I point to the unmade bed. "This was a mistake."

"A mistake? I don't understand. I thought we had a great connection. I've wanted to be with you for so long. I thought you wanted to be with me too."

"It would never work with you and me. There are just too many issues."

"Jackson, I know we have a lot to deal with, but *together,* you and I can face anything."

"I'm too OCD to have someone live with me."

"What about you and Trace? You lived with him and made it work."

"I wasn't in love with Trace."

He narrows his eyes. "So you admit you are in love with me?"

Hearing his words, I'm caught off guard. "I didn't say that, Eli." God, how do I get out of this mess? "I…I just need some time." There's no going back now. I take a deep breath and storm ahead. "We're not a couple. We'll never be a couple. Got it?"

The damage I'm doing to him is evident on his face, but he doesn't say a word.

God, it's killing me but this is the best thing for him. "As soon as your apartment is ready I think you need to go back home."

"If that's how you feel, I'm not waiting until it's ready," he says in a tone that rumbles with frustration.

I watch him cross the hall and start packing his clothes. "You don't have to leave right this minute. That's not what I meant."

"I don't care if you meant it or not. I'm still going." He's angry and hurt, but as much as I wish I could change this—I can't. "When my place is done I'll come back for the rest of my things."

I watch him storm out of the guest bedroom and walk down the stairs. When I hear my front door slam, the tears stream down my face.

Chapter 11

Since Eli left, my brain just won't shut down. I keep going over and over everything that happened between us. No answers. None. One minute I feel like I've made a mistake. The next I'm sure I did the right thing—*for Eli*.

Seeing the time on my phone, I realize I need to shake this blue mood off. My tennis match starts in thirty minutes.

Rushing out my backdoor, I notice Eli's car is gone. Where did he go? To the fire station? Back to the hospital to see Scott?

As more questions swirl inside me, I jump into my car. Turning the key, the engine starts and my phone syncs with the radio. I open up my iTunes library. As I drive out of the parking lot, Adele's latest song blasts through the speakers ripping my heart to shreds. I should change it to a more uplifting song, but I don't. Adele's painful lyrics and haunting melody are also *syncing* with what I'm feeling.

Just before I arrive at campus, I switch on Pharrell's song about being happy, recalling Aunt Jenny's admonishment when I was younger "Fake it 'til you make it, Jackson." I don't want to be a total wreck when I play my match.

Unfortunately, my mood doesn't change. I just keep thinking about Eli.

When I get to the tennis courts, Brad and the coach are waiting for me. There are more spectators than I expected, likely due to the warm weather. Several people are still arriving and going into the stands.

The opposing team that Brad and I will be playing doubles with is warming up. We've played them before and barely eked out a win. God, I've got to get my head in the game. But is that even possible today?

"You're late, Jackson," Coach says with a frown.

"Sorry, Coach."

"You and Brad need to warm up fast. Your match starts in five minutes." He walks over to another court where our other teammates are already playing.

"Hey, don't let him get under your skin." Brad sends me a wink and heads to the other side of the net. "We're going to win this, sweetheart."

Sweetheart? Damn it. Not that again. That's the last thing I need to deal with.

We volley the ball for our five minutes and then the match starts.

We twirl a racquet and the chose up. The W on the end of the handle lands right side up. They choose to serve first.

The first guy serving delivers an ace at my feet.

"15-love," the referee announces.

"That's okay, honey," Brad whispers to me. "We've got this."

I wish he would stop calling me that.

Another ace.

"Damn it," Brad curses softly.

"30-love."

I take a deep breath, readying myself for the serve. "He's good."

"But not as good as you," Brad says.

"Just keep your head in the game," I say to him and to myself.

The guy throws the ball in the air and swings his racquet. The ball tips the net but lands in the service area.

"Let."

Getting focused on the game is helping my mood much better

than the music. It forces me to focus all my attention. I bend my knees, watching intensely the movements of the guy serving.

His next serve, the ball sails past the net, landing legally. I take a single step to my left and with my backhand return the ball. The other player tries to slap it back, but the ball hits the net.

"30-15."

Brad misses the next serve.

"40-15. Game point."

Head in the game, Jackson. Head in the game. Don't think about Eli.

I miss the next serve.

"Game."

Brad comes over. "That's okay, Jackson. We're good."

We lose four more games before I find my rhythm but we still lose the set, winning only three. The second set, I set the court on fire and Brad really steps up his game as well. We finish out the set winning six and giving up two. The third set is tighter at 6-4, with us ending up with the win.

The final set comes in at 6-0 and we win the match.

We shake our opponents' hands and Brad, of course, has to come close and hug me.

He steps back, smiles and scans the crowd. "What a great turnout to watch us slaughter them." Suddenly, he frowns, which surprises me. One thing constant about Brad is he loves attention.

"What's the matter?"

"Nothing." He puts his arm around my shoulder. "Let's head to the locker room, champ."

Champ is better than sweetheart. At least there is some improvement.

"And I want to buy you a beer. What do you say?"

"No, Brad."

"Oh, come on. We just won our match. You can't say no."

"I believe I already did."

"Jackson, I know we left things awkward last night, but just give me a chance. I'm crazy about you. Can't you see that? Imagine what it will be like with me. I can buy you anything you want. The sky is the limit. Let me take care of you."

Frustrated, I shake my head. "How can I make it crystal clear to you that we are not nor ever will be a couple? Why isn't it sinking in, Brad?" Because he's rich, I bet he's always gotten whatever he wants. But this is one guy he's not getting. "I don't have those kind of feelings for you and never will."

"How can you possibly say that when you haven't even given me a chance? It's that fireman, isn't it? Eli Grayson."

"I'm not going to argue with you about this anymore." I turn around and head to my car.

God, why did Brad have to mention his name? My mood, which had lifted some during the tennis match, slams back down into that dark place.

I just need to get out of here and keep my appointment with Harvey. He always gives great advice for times like these.

When I park in front of my mom's house, I see Harvey hasn't arrived. Glancing at the time, I realize I'm a few minutes early.

Realizing it's been months since I've been here, I walk to the same door that Dave the EMT carried mom out years ago. That moment is seared in my brain forever, fresh as the day it happened. I put the key in the lock and open the door. It swings wide. There's nothing left inside to block it. The place was completely emptied out after she died. But the odor that spews out gags me and makes my eyes burn. I lift my T-shirt over my nose and rush to open every window.

Oh, God. I don't want Harvey to smell this. He doesn't know about Mom. I pull out my phone, hoping to cancel the appointment, but I see through the window that he's already parking his truck behind my car. *Too late. Damn.*

Maybe I can head him off. I run out the door and see him walking up the sidewalk with his toolbox.

"Harvey, I think it's best we cancel."

"Okay, son. But I really think I should check on that stench. I bet an animal has gotten inside and died. Needs to be taken care of ASAP."

This house is just a part of the baggage I don't want to bring into Eli's life. I won't. As hard as it is for me to open up, I realize it isn't fair to keep Harvey in the dark any longer.

"There's no dead animal, Harvey. At least I don't think there is. But there's something I should have told you a long time ago about the house and about my mom. It's one of the reasons I've kept rescheduling. If you don't want to take this project on, I'll understand."

Harvey's eyes narrow. "What are you talking about, Jackson? I'm perfectly fine with this job. I want to help you."

"Thanks, but it's just that…this is really hard to say."

"Just spit it out. You know I love you. Love all you kids like you were my own. You and I don't need any secrets between us."

"No, we don't." I take a deep breath. "My mom was a hoarder. That's why there is a smell."

"Well, don't worry about a thing. We can take care of that right away."

"Thanks, Harvey. You always know how to put people at ease. The good thing is all the junk is cleared out. Aunt Jenny and I hired a crew right after mom died." I take a deep breath. "Let's not cancel. I've been putting this off for far too long."

"Good deal." He winks at me. "I have a few tricks up these old sleeves. Hold on, Jackson." He sits down his toolbox and goes to his truck. When he comes back he has two paint masks and two pairs of gloves. He gives me one pair and a mask and puts the others on himself. "A guy in my line of work always has to be prepared, so this will help with the odor."

I place the mask and gloves on and we walk inside Mom's house.

"We need to rip out these carpets," Harvey says, bending down in the corner of the living room, pulling up the edge of the rug. "Look at the wood floor under this. Once these are refinished they will look amazing. I bet the whole house has hardwood under all the carpet."

As we look through the rest of the place, Harvey takes measurements and jots down notes. Having him with me in Mom's house is making me feel a little better about things.

"Do you know where the crawl space is to get into the attic?" he asks me.

"There's a pull-down in the hallway right in front of my old bedroom door." As I lead him to it, I remember mom filling the attic to the brim, going up and down the ladder with her arms loaded with boxes. The crew who cleared out the place charged us an extra fee for that space.

I tug on the string and unfold the ladder until it's resting at our feet. Harvey heads up first and I follow behind.

"There's a light switch to your left," I tell him. "I have kept the utilities on for the entire year. The plan has always been to fix up the place and put it on the market. I doubt I'll make much, but whatever I do will go to helping me with grad school."

"Grad school, Jackson?" Harvey flips the switch and the 100-watt light bulb illuminates the attic. "What degree you going for?"

"I want to be a psychologist. I want to help people like my mom. I've thought about it for a long time but I've finally made up my mind this very moment. That's what I want to do."

"Congratulations, Jackson."

"For what? I've still got years of grad school ahead of me."

"For making up your mind. Most young people don't have a clue what they want to do today." He opens up the side of the heater and AC unit. "Oh, boy."

"I don't like the sound of that. How much to fix it?"

"Doesn't look like it can be fixed, sorry to say. It's rusted and the wires are chewed through. I won't know for sure until I spend some time with it though."

"How much if I have to replace it?"

The number he quotes is much lower than I expected. "Harvey, that's not going to be enough, is it?"

"You're getting the Harvey Special, kid. I get discounts with my suppliers, and I always pass them down to my family members. After all, I've got more money than I can ever spend. I do this kind of work because I love it. Just like you'll love helping people once you get your psychology degree. That gives me an idea. I should introduce you to Nathan. He's a retired psychologist."

"Nathan?"

"You remember. The guy I went out with last night." Harvey smiles broadly.

"By the look on your face I bet it went quite well."

"Oh it did. Very well. I had a wonderful time. He's charming and smart and...romantic." Harvey pulls out his phone. "I took a selfie with him. Take a look."

Even though Harvey is approaching eighty, I'm not surprised he uses the term "selfie" instead of "took a photo." He's just like S & M, up to date in every way. The guy next to Harvey on the screen reminds me a little of Malcolm, same white hair and blue eyes.

"You two look adorable together."

"We do, don't we. We're going out again tonight. Nathan is taking me downtown for a steak dinner at Pyles' newest restaurant."

"Fancy. I like this guy already."

"So do I, Jackson. So do I. Take it from me, when you find the right guy, don't hesitate. Jump in with both feet. I hesitated once, and I'll always regret it."

My mind immediately brings up the image of Eli as he storms out of my apartment. "Even if you think you're protecting the other person?"

"Mm. That's a tough one." Harvey shakes his head. "The bottom line is I don't think anyone has the right to make a decision for another person unless they ask for advice. All a guy should do is follow his own heart."

"Maybe you're right." Did I make a mistake with Eli, pushing him away? Is it too late to fix things with him if I did?

"Jackson, love isn't always easy. In fact, it can be very messy, but trust a guy who has lived a very long time and seen a whole lot of things. Love is always worth it."

I smile. "Well, this young man knows a few things too."

"Oh, really? What things?"

"The most important is that we better hurry and finish up here since you have a hot date with Nathan tonight."

"Right you are. Let's check out the water heater and then we'll go. Where's is it?"

"In a closet right off the kitchen."

As we go down the attic ladder, I can't stop thinking about Eli. Like Harvey's Nathan, Eli is charming, smart, and romantic. Could there be a chance at something real between us, something that lasts?

Once in the kitchen, Harvey opens the closet door and begins inspecting the water heater. "What's this?" He bends down and reaches behind the tank. "Got it." He pulls out the skeleton of what is obviously a cat that's been dead a very long time.

"Oh my God, Harvey. I'm so sorry you had to see this."

"Hey, it's okay. No big deal. Just a cat."

"Not just a cat. One of mom's cats. After CPS made me leave, she started feeding every stray cat in the neighborhood. Just more things for her to collect."

The old shame rises up inside me. No sleepovers. No visitors. No one should see this. Not Harvey. Not Eli. *Especially not Eli.* I'm not good enough for him. But Harvey just told me that I shouldn't make decisions for other people. Is he right? Instead of pushing Eli away should I open up and let him see all of me? All of my baggage?

Once Eli knows everything, will he still want me? That's my real problem, isn't it? I'm terrified that he wants me, but I'm also terrified that when he sees this and knows everything that he won't want me. Either way, I will end up hurting him. That's the last thing I want to happen.

But should I listen to Harvey and at least try? I just don't know.

Chapter 12

When I drive back into my parking space at Mockingbird Place, I see Eli's car. He's the last person I want to talk to, but dammit I need to go see him more than anything.

Not a good idea, Jackson. Not one bit.

As I get out of my car, I remind myself about the condition of mom's house and realize there is no chance for Eli and me. I have so much baggage to deal with. I should stay away from him.

Here I go again. Making Eli's decision for him. God, I'm so confused. I'm a total mess.

I walk inside my back door and immediately open a bottle of wine. After pouring myself a glass, I sit down on the sofa and start listening to sad songs again, making me miss Eli even more.

I've got to turn my mood around. I need a distraction, but my place is perfectly neat and tidy. Nothing else I can do comes to mind. Usually, that doesn't stop me from picking up a dust rag or a mop. But I'm in no mood to clean, realizing that it's not going to help me one bit this time. So I go upstairs to take a shower. Once in the bathroom, I start Taylor Swift's song to try to help shake off this pity party I'm having. I'm normally not the guy who wallows in self-pity, so I turn her music up loud and jump in the shower. Aunt Jenny's sage words of advice ring in my ears. *Fake it 'til you make it.* So as loud as I can, I start singing with Taylor.

After I turn off the water, my black mood hasn't changed much. I still hate how I left things with Eli when we parted. I walk out of the bathroom to get my clothes from my bedroom and see him coming up the stairs.

"Hey." Eli's voice is as sexy as ever, but his face is dark and stormy.

"Hey," I say back to him, trying to act nonchalant.

"Just here to get the rest of my things." He walks past me into the guest bedroom.

"Okay." God, this is as awkward as it gets since I'm standing here totally naked. I step back into the bathroom and grab my towel, wrapping it around my waist.

When I hear him taking his things out of the closet, my heart screams at me to go in there and tell him to not to leave. I close my eyes, willing myself to stay put. I should offer to help him but I wouldn't be able to bear being in the same room with him.

I've got to get out of here while he's moving his things. I yell, "Hey, Eli, I've got an errand to run. Do you mind locking up when you're done?"

"Not necessary, since I'm leaving now." With his arms full of clothes, Eli steps out of the bedroom and looks me straight in the eyes. "I don't know what is making you act like such an asshole, Jackson. What are you really afraid of? Us? We're perfect for each other, even if you're too blind to see it. I know we are. But I'm not an idiot or a fool or a beggar. I've made it clear how I feel about you. So if you want your key, you come and get it. I'm done."

Before I can say a word, he storms down the stairs and out the front door, once again.

Stunned and devastated, I feel like the life I always wanted just blew up in my face. What have I done? I certainly screwed up this time. It's over—over before we even got a chance to really begin. Damn it. I made a mistake. Hell, I don't know what I'm doing.

My phone rings.

"Hi, Aunt Jenny."

"Jackson, did you win your match?"

"Yes."

"Congratulations. Did you keep the appointment with Harvey today?"

"I did."

"Oh, I'm so glad. I know that had to be hard."

"Yeah, it was." I sigh. "He found a skeleton of a cat behind the water heater."

"Honey, I'm sorry. Why don't you come over? I just pulled some chocolate chip cookies out of the oven that are just dying to be eaten. I'll put on a pot of coffee to go with them and you and I can have one of our good old heart to hearts."

"That's sounds delicious and wonderful." I love Aunt Jenny. She's always ready to listen to me and I definitely need to talk to her. "I'll be there in fifteen minutes."

I turn off the main road into Aunt Jenny's neighborhood, which is one of the nicest in Dallas. When I park in front of her house, I see her standing in the doorway waiting for me. She waves and motions me forward as I step out of the car.

As I walk up to her, I take a long hard look at the place that was also my home for a few years. It's a ranch-style house that Uncle Bill built for her. He died when I very young, but I remember his broad smile. The house has a long porch and a big bay window. Inside are three bedrooms, two and a half baths, and a den with a fireplace. A photo of Uncle Bill in his military uniform sits on the mantle to this very day. My favorite room and the heart of the home was always—and still is—the kitchen. That's where Aunt Jenny works her magic, creating the most delicious meals in the world and lending her ear to me whenever I need her—like now.

"Come here and give your old aunt a hug, Jackson." She spreads her arms wide.

As I always do, I pick her up and spin her around, which isn't difficult. She's only five-one and can't weigh more than a hundred and ten pounds fully dressed. She has bright blue eyes and long dark brown hair.

"Do you see I'm wearing the apron you bought me for Christmas from your lawn mowing money?"

I lower her to her feet and step back. "Aunt Jenny, that was years ago. I think it's time I bought you a new one."

"If I wore a different apron my cookies wouldn't taste as good, sweetheart." She smiles. "Let's go and sit down at the table. I'll get our coffee and cookies and then we can have a good long talk."

Taking my seat, I wonder if she and Eli would hit it off if they ever met. I'm sure they would. But that's never going to happen. Not now. Not after I've ruined everything.

She places a tray of cookies in the middle of the table and hands me a cup of coffee. "Okay," she says, sitting in the chair across from me. "We're all set. Tell your old aunt what's on your mind."

"Old? Aunt Jenny, you're only fifty-one. That's not old. In fact, it's time you started going on some dates."

She grins. "Who says I haven't?"

"What?"

"I decided it was time to move on. My Bill has been gone for many years now. And I get a little lonely since you moved out. So I put up a profile on a dating site. I've had three coffee dates already. What do you think about that?"

I grab her hand. "I think that's marvelous, Aunt Jenny."

"I'm glad to hear you say that because I think it's time for you to put up a profile too. Your mom has been gone for a year now, Jackson, and it's been ages since you've dated. Who did you go out with last?"

I shrug. "Trace, actually, if you mean a proper date."

She shakes her head. "Trace. That's what I figured. And you two are like brothers now. What do you say? Shall I get my laptop?"

"Actually, that's what I want to talk to you about. There is a guy I'm interested in but I made a complete mess of things." I sigh. "I really blew my chance with him."

"What do you mean you blew it? As nice and kind as you are I can't imagine you blowing it."

"But I did, Aunt Jenny. Maybe it's for the best though. I have so much crap from my past. A good guy like Eli doesn't deserve a person who leaves when things get rough."

"What the hell are you talking about, Jackson? That's not you."

"Yes, it is. I left mom and she died."

"Oh, honey, you didn't leave her. Your mom had a choice to clean up her house or CPS was going to take you, but she didn't. You were a minor. You didn't have a choice."

"Maybe not then, but when I turned eighteen I could have moved back in with her instead of going to Mockingbird Place. Maybe I could have gotten through to her. Maybe she would still be here if I had made the right decision."

"Sweetheart, when are you going to let this go? You've suffered with this far too long. Your mom was ill. That's all. If anyone is too blame it's me. I was the adult. I should have had her committed. I just didn't have the courage." Aunt Jenny looks at me with her loving eyes. "So if you want to blame someone, blame me."

"I could never blame you. You're the one who never stopped trying to help her or me. You've sacrificed so much. It's just that I—"

"Stop it, Jackson. Stop punishing yourself. There was nothing you or I could do. Nothing. I know it. I begged her time and again. I offered to come over and help, but as you know she never would let me inside. I even hired a crew back then to help your mom, but she turned them away."

"But as her son I should have been there." I feel my eyes stinging with bitter tears. "She was alone, Aunt Jenny. All alone."

"Your mom wouldn't want to see you suffering like this." She puts her hand on top of mine. "Now listen, young man. You need to hear this. I called your mother the day before the deadline CPS had set for her about the house. I thought I would try one more time to get through to her. But I could hear the resignation in her voice. She told me how worried she was about you, but every time she tried to throw out one little thing she went into a panic. And she knew that living with her was dangerous for you. As hard as it was on her for you to leave, she had no other choice and knew it was for the best."

"Why didn't you tell me about that phone call?"

She looks down at her hands, clearly struggling with the memory. "You were only fifteen and wouldn't have understood. When you moved into Mockingbird Place, your mom was thrilled. Don't you remember how she hung on every word you told her about all of your wonderful neighbors? You're wrong, Jackson. Moving in with her when you turned eighteen wouldn't have changed anything. You living out in the world and thriving was the one bright spot in her life." Tears fall down Aunt Jenny's cheeks. "I was the one at fault, Jackson, not you. I wish I'd had the courage to have her committed. She was my sister. It was just too hard. But that was the only thing I hadn't tried. Nothing else worked."

I lean over and wrap my arms around her. "Now who needs to stop feeling guilty?"

"Me and you. God, I miss your mom."

"Me, too. But you're right, we both need to stop playing the what-if game, don't we?"

She wipes her eyes. "Yes, we do. Now, tell me about Eli. He's the fireman at the complex, right?"

I nod, and recount everything that happened between him and me. "I pushed Eli away, Aunt Jenny. And now I feel like whatever chance we might have had is gone."

"Sweetheart, I don't believe that. You said his last words to you were that if you wanted your key you could come and get it."

"But then he said he was done."

"You clearly don't get what he meant, do you? He means the ball is in your court now. He told you that you were perfect for each other but he wasn't going to beg. He's done. It's your turn now. That's why he held on to your key. You have to come and get it." She grins. "Get it?"

"Oh, my God, you're right. That's what he meant. I thought he was through with me."

"How could anyone be through with that gorgeous face?"

I stand and kiss her on the forehead. "Thank you so much, but I've got to go find Eli."

Chapter 13

On the drive back to Mockingbird Place, I turn off Adele and turn on Pharrell. It's easy to sing his lyrics about being happy. I am happy. I want Eli. Aunt Jenny helped me see the light. We still have a chance. When Eli held onto my key, he left the door wide open. And I intend to walk through it.

I'm thrilled to see his car in his assigned space when I pull into the parking lot. But the very next second doubts blast at my resolve. He's probably still very pissed. He may not even open the door. But I have to give it a try. I just have to.

Stepping out of my car, I take a deep breath, determined to push through my anxiety. I force my legs to step to his door—one foot in front of the other.

When I get to his door, I hesitate. What am I afraid of? If Eli says he doesn't want to have anything to do with me at least I tried. But that's exactly what I *am* afraid of. Wouldn't it be better to just let things cool down for a bit?

Before I can back off his step and walk to my place, the door opens.

"I thought I heard someone out here." Eli stands right in front of me, leaving me nowhere to hide.

"Hi." The single syllable word that leaves my lips sounds shaky to me. Can he tell how nervous I am?

"I suppose you came for your key." The anger I felt coming off of him earlier is just as hot now as it was then.

No backing down now, no matter what happens. "I actually came for more than that, Eli. Can we talk?"

"Yes. You can come in. I have a lot I need to say to you, if you'll listen." He backs up into the apartment and motions me inside. "Sorry, I don't have any chairs for us. I've been sitting on this blanket."

"I told you that you didn't have to leave, Eli."

"I know you didn't say that exactly, but I felt like I wasn't welcome anymore at your place. And if I did stay it would have been very awkward."

The edge in his voice concerns me. Will I be able to convince him that I made a mistake and that I want to be with him now? Can I fix things between us? God, I have to. I just have to.

He points to the blanket on the floor. "My sofa for now."

I take a seat, not sure how to begin this conversation.

Eli gets down next to me.

"This is kind of like having a picnic, isn't it?" I ask, hoping to break the tension.

"I guess it is. I'm supposed to get the check from the insurance company Tuesday. That's when I'll go furniture shopping. But aren't we just dancing around the real issue?"

"Yeah, but I'm nervous."

"Why be nervous? I'm no different than I was before you made it clear that you weren't interested in me."

"That's just it. I am interested but I was being an idiot."

"Okay then. What is your problem?"

I can tell he's not convinced that I've had a change of heart. I can't blame him. I keep sending him mixed signals. That's got to stop. How do I get him to see why I acted like I did when I don't fully know myself? "Would you believe I lost my mind for a little bit? Temporary insanity?"

"Yeah. I can believe that."

"I'm a control freak, Eli. I told you about my mom being a hoarder."

"Yes, you did, but I don't see how that relates to us."

"Let me explain. I will never live in a place like she did again. After CPS took me out of her home, I ended up swinging the pendulum the opposite way. I am obsessive about neatness. It's hard to live with me. Just ask Trace. When you and I got closer, I flipped out. I worried that you might not be able to handle my compulsion for cleanliness. I was afraid that if I opened up to you any more that we were headed for a total mess and both of us would end up hurt. So, I decided to wipe the slate clean before we ended in a place where we couldn't at least be friends. Selfish and stupid, I know. But I got scared. That's the truth."

"There's more to it than that. What about your feelings about Scott and me?"

"You're right. That bothered me at first. I never thought of myself as a jealous person but it turns out I am. But I get it now, especially since you told me that the two of you were never really a couple. He's in trouble. And you're the kind of man who shows up when people need help. But even then I worried. Mental illness is something that takes its toll on everyone—the one suffering with it and those around who care. Scott is going to be in your life from now on. That's the truth. But I'm learning to be okay with that, Eli. I want you, and if that means I need to stand by your side to help him, that's where I want to be."

"Are you sure that's all, Jackson? There's nothing else?"

His question cuts through me like a knife and nearly reaches something deep and dark within me. A secret fear I've been running from my whole life. I'm not ready to face that demon. Besides, that has nothing to do with him and me. I just want him. I shove the nightmare back down, and say, "That's all. Nothing else."

"The way you pushed me away was very hard, Jackson. It hurt. And your timing sucked. I've been dumped before but never right after sex."

"God, I'm so sorry. I just freaked out, Eli. I had all these mixed feelings about you and Scott, and then my own baggage hit me right in the face. It's no excuse but it is how I felt."

His stare is unwavering, making me uneasy. But I don't look away. "How do you feel now, Jackson?"

"That's what I'm trying to say. I want to be with you. I want to give *us* a chance."

"The only way that I'll open the door is if we go very slow. I'm not going through that again."

"What do you mean slow? How slow?"

"I think we should start with simply dating. Think old fashioned, if you know what I mean."

"I know exactly what you mean, but that doesn't mean I have to like it, does it?"

He laughs and puts his arm around me. "I don't like it either, but that's how it needs to be for now."

"You got a deal." I kiss him, loving the taste of his lips on mine. "Too fast?"

"Yes, but we can make exceptions here and there." He grins.

"Eli, would you be my date to the gay rodeo to see Luke compete?"

"I'd be honored."

Chapter 14

I walk out of my favorite class this semester. Forensic Psychology. The professor and I are always on the same page, but today I just couldn't concentrate on the test. The only thing on my mind is going to the gay rodeo in Fort Worth with Eli. I'm not sure what kind of grade I'll end up with, but I still think I'll be able to get an A for the class.

I look down at the T-shirt and jeans I have on. Fine for today but not for tonight. Before I left this morning, I laid out what I'd spent all of Sunday shopping for. Western shirt. Levi's. Leather belt. And cowboy boots and hat.

I walk to the bench where Ava and I always meet after class. It's been great carpooling with her. She's become a very close friend.

Before I get to the bench, I see her walking toward me from the other direction. She speeds up, her long dark hair blowing behind her. I race to be the first to arrive at the bench. It's an impromptu contest we've been having this semester.

She plops down on the bench before I do. "I win." She laughs, her green eyes sparkling with victory.

I grin. "You cheated."

"How could I have cheated?"

"I don't know but you had to have cheated, Ava."

She playfully sticks out her tongue. "Jackson, you are a sore loser."

"That's me." I hug her. "Do you mind if we forgo the stop at Starbucks on the way home? I'm anxious to get ready for tonight."

She stands. "Do you really need five hours to get ready? I'm the one Luke and Trace always accuse of taking too long in the bathroom, and I certainly don't need five hours."

I leave the bench, and we start walking to the parking lot, which is five minutes away. "It's so important to me because I want this date with Eli to be perfect."

"Can't we discuss this in the Starbucks drive-thru? I really want my coffee. I was up so late with little Mick last night and I have lots of studying to do after we get home from the rodeo. Besides, I give my most sage advice when I'm caffeinated."

"Okay. You win again."

"That's two for me and zero for you, Jackson."

"Don't rub it in. I have a great excuse. I'm very distracted and nervous today." I tell her about the outfit I came up with for the rodeo date with Eli. "I'm questioning the cowboy hat I bought yesterday. Is that going over the top? I'm no cowboy. Far from it. I'm city, all the way."

"Eli is from Abilene, Jackson. Being from West Texas myself, I'm sure he would love seeing you in a cowboy hat. I know I will."

"Are you sure?" I ask as we step over to my car.

"I'm absolutely positive. Besides, I think everyone is wearing cowboy hats to the rodeo—me, Trace, little Mick, and Luke for sure. I even got to take a look at Chad's cowboy hat." She grins, and we get inside my car. "Never seen anything like it. Green with tassels."

I laugh. "But what if Eli doesn't wear one? He'll feel left out."

"Calm down. I'm sure he will. He's from Abilene. This can't be his first rodeo. Tonight is going to be great. You have nothing to worry about."

"That's easy for you to say. You're not the one who nearly blew it with Eli. I am."

"Jackson, you told me this morning that you two already worked things out. Just breathe."

I nod and start the engine. Before I turn to look over my shoulder to pull out of the space, I spot Brad's black SUV right in front of us. He's behind the wheel glaring at me.

"What the hell? Why is he looking at me that way?"

"He seems like he would love to beat the crap out of you. Is that Brad?"

"Yep. Turns out he has a crush on me."

"No kidding," she says sarcastically. "Everyone knows that."

"I didn't. He wants more from me than I'm willing to give him."

"He looks really pissed, Jackson," she says with her voice full of concern. "You are staying away from this guy?"

Before I can answer, Brad backs his car out of the spot and races away, screeching his tires.

Ava turns to me. "You need to let the university know about this. He could be dangerous."

"I'm not comfortable doing that. He's just upset. It will be okay."

"But he may run over somebody acting like that," she says. "Oh, look. The campus police are pulling him over now."

I see the flashing lights. "Good. It will give Brad time to cool down."

"But why was he so mad at you? Don't you think that's weird?"

"Yes, I do. Very strange. Very weird. But I haven't a clue. Well... maybe I do."

"Spill it then."

"He asked me to go to Banff with him this summer but I turned him down. I tried to make it clear to him then that we were never going to be together. But he just wouldn't listen. So after our doubles match on Saturday, he started calling me 'sweetheart' and 'honey' and giving me hugs. I had to be very firm. He didn't take it well, and I haven't talked to him since."

Ava nods. "I'm getting the picture nice and clear now. Just be careful around him."

"That's odd. Brad said the same thing to me about Eli."

"Of course he would. That guy is jealous of you two." She grabs my hand. "Unlike you and Brad, you and Eli do belong together."

"Maybe we do, but Eli and I are taking it slow."

She smiles. "Trust me, you two will be in the fast lane before you know it."

"I hope you're right." I squeeze her hand and look her directly in her eyes. "But for now, you need your coffee and I need to get home to get ready for my date. The police have things well in hand."

"I agree." In a British accent, she adds, "To the Starbucks, my dear Jackson, if you please."

I laugh and back out of the space.

AS I GET ready for my date with Eli, I make a promise to myself not to blow it again. I'm very nervous, although it feels so good to be going out with him. Not your typical date, but no one who lives at Mockingbird Place follows typical paths. We're all unique. So on this date we'll be chaperoned by our neighbors who are going to the rodeo with us. I'm glad. With them around I'll have less of a chance to say the wrong thing to him.

Fully dressed in the outfit I chose for the date with Eli and holding my new black felt Stetson in my left hand, I stare at my reflection in the mirror. "I'll fit in at the rodeo just fine, but will Eli like how I look?" I place the hat on my head. "Should I wear the hat? No. I don't think so." I take it off. "Well, maybe." I put it back on. "Damn, I don't know what to do."

My phone rings. It's Ava. I answer it.

"Wear the hat, Jackson. Just wear the damn hat."

I hear the click and pull the phone away from my ear. Stunned, I stare at the screen. "That girl just said her piece and then hung up on me." I grin, realizing she wanted to make a point and give me no chance to argue. "How the hell did she know I was trying on the hat? I swear that girl has psychic powers."

I take one last glance at my reflection with the hat on.

"Okay, Ava. I hope you're right." I grab my keys and head downstairs and out the door to Eli's place.

I push the button and hear his doorbell ring inside.

Eli opens the door and smiles. "Well hello, handsome. Jackson you look great."

He stands in front of me sexy as hell in a black Western shirt, bolo tie, tight jeans, and cowboy boots. But no hat. *Damn.*

"You're the one who looks great, Eli. You ready to go?"

"Hold on just a second." He rushes up his stairs.

I wonder what he forgot. I take off the hat, wishing I had left it behind.

When Eli gets back to the door, he's wearing a cowboy hat. "Now I'm ready. I'm so glad you had a cowboy hat on. I was torn whether to wear mine or not. This is Dallas, after all. Not Abilene."

I kiss him. "I was torn, too. But now I'm not, thanks to you." I place the hat on my head. "Let's ride, cowboy."

Arm in arm we walk to the parking lot, and to our shock find Scott getting out of his white BMW.

"Eli, did he get released?"

"I don't know but I'm going to find out."

Scott frowns when he sees Eli and I together and then walks over to us. "Hi, Eli."

"What's going on, Scott?" Eli asks him. "I thought you were still in the hospital."

Never looking my direction, all of Scott's attention is on Eli. "I only came to tell you good-bye and ask you for a favor. I know you've already been taking care of Vader while I've been in the hospital, and I hate to spring this on you, but I need a bigger favor."

Eli turns to me. "Vader is his cat. Where are you going, Scott?"

"The doctors at the hospital set it up for me to go to a dual diagnostic facility in Austin next to Lake Travis."

"The Thompson Center?" I ask.

He turns his head and glares at me. "Yes. The Thompson Center." He looks back at Eli. "I don't know how long I will be gone. So I was wondering if Vader could stay with you until I get back? I can't bear to give him away."

"Of course he can stay here. You know I love Vader. No problem."

"That's a relief." Scott sighs. "Thank you so much, Eli. That takes a load off of my mind."

"I'll pick him up tomorrow."

"My doctor thinks that the Thompson Center will be the best place for me to get the long-term help that I need. I don't know if they're right, but I have to try. Eli, you know how difficult it's been for me. I'm tired of feeling this way."

Scott sounds sincere, but I have to wonder if this is just another attempt to manipulate Eli. It doesn't feel like that to me, but what is still crystal clear is Scott doesn't like me being around Eli.

"That's great." Eli smiles. "Really great. Do you know how long you'll be gone?"

"No. They say I can stay until the doctors there are sure I'm fine."

Eli hugs him. "I'm proud of you, buddy. And your brother would be too. Please keep in touch and let me know how it's going."

Scott steps closer to him. "I was hoping we could have dinner before I leave."

"I can't," Eli says. "Jackson and I have a date tonight. How about breakfast tomorrow?"

Scott shakes his head. "I'm hitting the road tonight. They're expecting me at the center after midnight. Can't you reschedule your date with him?"

Realizing that going to the center is a big step for Scott, I say, "If you want to pick another time, Eli, I'll understand."

"No, Jackson. We already bought the tickets." He turns back to Scott. "I'm sorry, but this is for the best. It's never good to have long good-byes."

"Okay, Eli. But I'm sure going to miss you." Scott hugs him and steps back, tears streaming down his cheeks. "I'm going to get better. I am."

He turns to me and the look of resignation is on his face. "Bye, Jackson. Take good care of him."

"I will do my best."

As we watch Scott get back in his BMW and drive away, I am filled with compassion for him. Even though his issues are different from my mom's, there are similarities. Scott lost his parents and his brother. Mom lost my dad and their baby. Crushing grief pushed both of them over the edge. Mom fixated on things. Scott on Eli. Mom didn't survive her illness. Maybe Scott will. At least he's able to try.

"God, I hope this works this time." Eli sighs. "He has so many demons to deal with."

I put my arm around him. "Yes, but thank God Scott is getting help."

Chapter 15

Sitting next to Eli in the stands with our friends, I feel the pace of my heartbeat speed up. I'm a nervous wreck waiting for Luke's turn in the bareback bronc-busting competition. After watching other cowboys in the same event hit the dirt hard, it's no wonder.

I keep glancing at Ava, who is sitting directly in the row in front of us between Trace and Harrison. She and Harrison are getting along quite well. It seems that Trace feels better about that situation after the talk we had the other night. But he and Ava are clearly nervous too as we wait to hear the announcer say Luke's name.

"I can't stand this, Trace." Ava grabs his hand. "Let's go tell Luke that he doesn't have to do this."

"We can't do that, Ava. You know how much he's been looking forward to this."

She shakes her head, pulling her hand back from him. "Well, if he breaks his arm or leg or ribs it's all on you. Little Mick won't understand when Luke isn't able to hold him."

I reach forward and place my hand on her shoulder. "It's going to be okay," I tell her in my most convincing tone.

She turns around. "You really think so?"

"We all have to remember this isn't Luke's first rodeo. Get it?"

Everyone chuckles and she smiles.

"I've seen him compete a few times, but those rodeos were before Mick died." Ava sighs. "This time just seems even more scary to me for some reason."

Lashaya leans over to her. "Of course it does, Ava. You're a mother now."

Lashaya sits between her husband Hayden and her brother Brexton, who has been living with them for the past few months.

"What does me being a mother have to do with how I'm feeling right now?" Ava asks her.

"Everything. That's what I've been learning in my parenting classes. Our protective nature really kicks into high gear after our babies arrive."

"I bet you're right, and I can't wait for your baby to arrive."

"I'm excited, anxious, and just a little bit scared, Ava. I want to be as good a mom as you are."

Hayden puts his arm around Lashaya. "It's going to be okay, sweetheart. In a few months, we'll have our little baby in our arms. You're going to make the best mommy ever."

Lashaya kisses him.

"Oh shucks, you two," Brexton says teasingly. "You are too cute for words, just like our new baby is going to be."

Eli leans over and whispers to me, "I think it will be great to have another little one to spoil at Mockingbird Place. Have you seen all the things S & M have bought for Mick and for Lashaya and Hayden's baby? They'll be the biggest spoilers of all of us."

"I know. Did you see how quickly they jumped at the chance to watch little Mick so Trace and Ava could come tonight?"

Before Eli can answer me, the announcer's voice booms from the speakers, "The next cowboy up is Luke Wagner from Dallas, Texas. He'll be riding Black Devil, a bronc that's notorious for bucking off competitors right out of the gate."

"Black Devil," Trace says, twisting his hands together over and over.

I place my other hand on his shoulder. "Just breathe, buddy. Just breathe."

Eli's squeezes my leg. "Take your own advice, Jackson. You're holding your breath."

The gate opens and Luke and the beast he's on top of come blasting out.

"From shoot number 2, Luke Wagner," the announcer shouts, as we all get to our feet. "Look at him ride."

Black Devil twists and turns and leaps into the air, trying to buck off Luke, but Mockingbird Place's favorite cowboy stays on until the 8-second buzzer goes off. Then he falls off the horse and lands on the ground. He immediately jumps up, waving to the crowd with his hat in his hand.

"Way to go, Luke!" Ava shouts. "I knew you could do it."

We all laugh, relieved that the ride went so well.

She turns and smiles at us. "Well, I did know. He's the best."

"We know, sweetheart." Harrison puts his arm around her and kisses her cheek.

Those two are definitely getting more serious.

It's a blast watching the rest of the events with Eli and everyone else. I can't remember having such a good time. Who knew I would like the rodeo? I certainly didn't. Watching Eli getting so excited adds to my enjoyment of being here. I smile, believing that he would make any event more fun for me.

When the award ceremony starts, I see Ava cross her fingers. We're all hoping to hear Luke's name. And we are not disappointed. He not only takes home the buckle for bareback riding but also gets the highest award for all-around cowboy.

"This night couldn't get any better," Eli says, wrapping his arms around my shoulders.

"Don't jinx it," I say with a grin.

"I never knew you were superstitious, Jackson."

"I didn't know it either, but I don't want to take a chance on anything ruining this perfect evening." I hold up my hands and cross my fingers. "It worked for Ava a moment ago. Luke won."

Eli laughs. "I think Luke won because he competed better than anyone else."

"I could fall in love with you right now, Mr. Fireman."

He holds up his hands and crosses his fingers. "Then do it."

A LITTLE PAST MIDNIGHT, I turn off the street into Mockingbird Place and immediately see something is on fire in the parking lot.

"Oh my God, Jackson, that's my car."

Flames and smoke are pouring out of Eli's Honda. I see Harvey run to the blaze with a water hose on full blast.

When I spot a man in a black hoodie running in the opposite direction, I hit the brakes, jump out, and chase the guy.

Eli must have seen him, too, because he's running beside me pulling out his phone.

The man ducks into the alley between Mockingbird Place and another apartment complex.

"Yes, we need the police and the fire department. A guy just set fire to my car and we are chasing him on foot now." Through fast breaths as we turn into the alley, Eli gives the 9-1-1 operator our address and current location. "No, ma'am. We do not want to lose sight of him." It's clear the operator doesn't want us chasing the man.

"We're too late, Eli. There's no sign of the guy."

Continuing to run down the alley, we keep searching for places the bastard might be hiding, but don't have any luck.

When we get to the next street that the alley intersects with, we stop.

Eli turns to me. "How in the hell did he get away from us?"

"He was fast."

We hear tires squealing in the next block past the stop sign.

A dark SUV is pealing away. I bring out my iPhone, click the camera icon, and hold down the button. I snap pictures until the vehicle is out of sight.

Still on the phone with 9-1-1, Eli tells the operator what we saw. "Yes, we're headed back now to my car."

We hear sirens off in the distance.

As we hurry back to the parking lot to help Harvey put out the blaze, Eli sighs. "There's no doubt now, is there?"

"No doubt about what?"

"The two fires, my apartment and my car, are not random acts. That runner is definitely after me, whoever he is."

"True, but it also proves Scott's innocence. He's on his way to Austin. Hell, he might already be at the Thompson Center by now."

When we get back to Eli's Honda, we see Harvey has already extinguished the blaze with the help of Jaris and Tony. Each of them holds a hose and continues to spray the car.

The sirens are getting louder.

Jaris spots us and yells, "Are you two okay?" Clearly he's in full-on doctor mode.

"We're fine," Eli answers.

Tony turns to us. "I saw you run after the creep who did this. Any luck?"

I come up beside him. "He got away, but luckily I got some pictures of his SUV."

Tony has a gash on his chin from his last MMA fight. The guy is lucky we didn't bring him back. Tony isn't the kind of guy who holds back when he's pissed, and it's obvious he's really pissed. So am I.

Eli nods. "Hopefully we'll get his license plate number from Jackson's pictures."

As more of our neighbors return from the rodeo in their vehicles, two police cars and a fire truck pull into the parking lot.

Seeing Captain Murphy get out of the fire truck and Detectives Soliz and Morrison exit one of the police cars, I feel like we're repeating what happened the other night. And Eli is the one who has lost something once again to an arsonist.

"Hello, gentlemen." The captain shakes Eli's hand. "I wish we were meeting under different circumstances."

"Me, too, Captain." Eli sighs. "Me, too."

"Looks like your neighbors acted quickly and took care of the fire. Not much left for my guys to do. They're just making sure it is totally out and there are no other issues."

"One of the easier calls," Eli says. "You'll be done here quick. I bet no more than fifteen minutes."

"That sounds about right, Grayson, but if you need me to stick around for moral support, I'm happy to do it."

"That's okay. I've got Jackson for that, don't I?"

"Yes, you do."

The captain nods. "Good to know. Grayson, don't worry about reporting to work any time soon. I know you have a lot to deal with."

"Actually, I'd like to get back to work. I need a little normalcy in my life. I can deal with anything else over the phone."

"I can help with whatever you need," I tell him.

The captain pats me on the back. "Looks like you're in good hands, Grayson. Tell you what, come by the station tomorrow morning and I'll let you know what schedule you're on."

"Thanks, Captain." Eli turns to the detectives. "We might have something that could help you. Jackson took some photos of the bastard's getaway car."

"How do you know it was the arsonist's car?" Soliz asks him.

"When he ran, Jackson and I chased after him. He ran into that alley over there." Eli points to it. "When we came out to the other street, an SUV was peeling out. It had to be his."

"Did you see the man get into the car?" Morrison asked.

"No, but it had to be him." I bring up the photos on my phone and hand it to Soliz.

"You may be right, but we'll need more than these photos," she says. "Unfortunately, I can't make out the plates. Too blurry."

"Damn. I was hoping I got one that would be clear. It happened so fast."

"We'll try to enhance the pictures and see if we can make out the license." She hands my phone back with her card. "Send these to my e-mail."

"I sure will. It looked like an SUV."

"Could you identify the make, model, or color?" Morrison asks us.

"No. Too dark and too fast. It looked new to me though."

"Definitely a late-model high-end SUV. Could have been a Mercedes or Infinity," Eli chimes in. "Maybe the pictures will identify the make."

"Mr. Grayson, do you know where Scott Foster is?" Soliz asks him.

"Scott did not do this," he snaps back. "He's in Austin."

"How do you know he's in Austin?"

"We saw him earlier, right here," Eli answers. "His car was packed. He was anxious to get on the road."

"He's checking into the Thompson Center for treatment." I can tell that Soliz and Morrison are not convinced. "Besides, he drives a white BMW. Not a dark SUV. Scott is innocent."

"It will be easy to verify he's there," Morrison says, stepping back and pulling out his phone.

We walk around Eli's car, which is a total loss.

"We'll check for prints," Soliz says. "The fire and the water will make that job difficult. We'll be very lucky if we find any usable prints."

Soliz takes down the rest of our statement.

Morrison steps over to us. "Just spoke with the nurse on-call at the Thompson Center. Foster is a no show."

I'm shocked to hear that Scott is missing. It's obvious so is Eli.

"Let me try his number," Eli says. "Damn it. It went straight to voicemail."

"Huh-uh." Morrison seems convinced Scott is the arsonist.

I'm just not so sure, though I'm concerned that Scott never arrived at the Thompson Center. Still, like Eli, I find it hard to believe he's the one responsible for this.

"Look, Detective," Eli says. "I've already told you. Scott didn't set this fire or the other fire. He's innocent. You need to focus your investigation on Jackson's photos. That guy is the one who is the arsonist."

"Mr. Grayson, where were you this evening?" Morrison asks as Eli's captain walks over to us.

"Oh, for crying out loud." Eli can't hide his frustration, not that he wants to. "Why in the world would I do this to my own self? I was at the gay rodeo in Fort Worth, Detective, with about fifteen of my friends. They're all here." He points to our neighbors gathered in the parking lot. "Just ask them yourself."

"We're just doing our jobs, Mr. Grayson," Soliz tells him. "We have to rule everything out."

"And everyone," Morrison adds.

"I get it. Sorry. It's just…this sucks."

"Detectives, are you done with my guy for now?" The captain puts his arm around Eli's shoulders.

"Yes," Soliz answers. "We'll be in touch."

She and Morrison head over to the forensic team. The area around Eli's car is already taped off.

"Don't worry, Eli. They're going to get to the bottom of this," Captain Murphy says. "With all the fires in the city, our chief, the police chief, and the mayor are giving high priority to any cases of arson. That's why you see so many officers here. Plus, this is the only location that has had two fires, and those only days apart."

"I sure hope you're right, Captain." Eli glances at his ruined car. "I just can't figure who in the world would be targeting me or why."

I look Eli in the eyes. "One thing for sure, you're staying at my place until the person responsible is caught and behind bars."

"I agree. I'd like some company tonight, and there's no one else I'd rather be with. Let me run over to my apartment and grab a few things."

There's no way I'm letting Eli out of my sight, not with a lunatic on the loose. "I'm coming with you."

We get to his door and find an envelope taped to it.

When Eli reaches for it, I grab his hand. "Wait. It might be from the arsonist. How many times have you had an envelope taped to your door?"

"Never."

"Exactly. Even if it's nothing, I think we should get Soliz first."

"You're right. Let's go get her."

When we tell Soliz about the envelope, she grabs a pair of gloves from one of the forensic officers.

"Morrison, we might have something." She motions for her partner to follow us.

Back at Eli's front door, Soliz puts on the gloves and removes the envelope. Carefully, she opens it, pulling out a single sheet of paper that is folded neatly.

"So? Is this from our guy or not?" Morrison asks her.

"I believe it is." She holds it out for all of us to read.

The words on the page send a shiver down my spine.

"Stay away from him or the next time somebody is going to get hurt."

Chapter 16

S tanding in the parking lot, I feel like Eli and I have been dropped into the middle of a TV police show. Sergeant Shaw, the lead forensic officer, is checking the envelope and note for fingerprints. Looking to be in his mid-50s, Shaw has a confident and warm manner about him, which reminds me a little of Harvey. With Shaw on the job, I can tell that he and his team are doing all they can to discover who the arsonist is. When Soliz brought Shaw the letter, he immediately went to work on it, leaving the rest of his team to finish checking Eli's car. Not wanting to miss a thing, we watch every move the sergeant makes as he carefully dusts the paper with a very fine powder.

Once done with his work, he places the envelope and note into an evidence bag.

"Any luck, Sergeant?" Soliz asks.

"No," Shaw answers flatly. "Nothing. The perp must have worn gloves when he wrote it."

The bastard who has it in for Eli clearly is no fool. He's careful and methodical. That will make catching him even harder. Did the arsonist know we were at the rodeo? If he did, how did he know?

I feel deflated, and Eli's eyes tell me he feels the same way. We were both hoping that the police would get closer to figuring out who is responsible. *Damn.* I wish we'd been able to catch up with the asshole in the alley.

"We'll check for DNA back at the lab, Detective." Shaw says to Soliz, placing the bag into his car. "If we're lucky, the guy licked the flap and we'll get a hit."

Hopefully, the creep didn't think of that, but I doubt it.

Soliz nods. "What about the car?"

"We're almost done, but so far we haven't found anything that we can use."

Just then, one of the female forensic officers says, "Got something, Shaw."

We follow him to the side of Eli's car.

"What did you get, Nichols?" Shaw asks her.

She shines a light source at the driver's side mirror. "Take a look."

He bends down. "Nice. We definitely were lucky with this one. Water and fire make a mess of latent prints," Shaw tells us.

Nichols hands the light to Shaw. "Let me lift this baby."

She uses a brush to spread powder on the glass.

"This is one of the good days," Shaw says. "Lady luck decided to smile at us. This reminds me of one of my early days on the force. A sexual assault occurred in one of the women's dorms at the university. I was the youngest on my team back then. The suspect was careful to not touch anything in the dorm room. But I noticed the toilet seat was up." Shaw smiles broadly. "Up? In a women's dorm?"

"Did you find a print on the seat?"

"No, but I did find a complete print of the perp's right hand on the wall behind the toilet. The bastard apparently left it while he leaned against the wall to take a piss after the assault. Because of his previous convictions, the judge sentenced him to the maximum."

Nichols steps back and Shaw shines the light once again on the mirror.

Even from where I'm standing, I can see the print. "There it is, Eli. Our first real break."

"Could be," Shaw says. "Or maybe this is Mr. Grayson's print or someone else's who has nothing to do with the fire. But at least it's something to look into."

As Nichols lifts the print, Morrison walks up to us. "Looks like you've had better luck than I have, Soliz."

"We got a print," she tells him. "Hopefully it's from the perp."

Morrison nods. "Still haven't been able to locate Mr. Foster."

Eli brings out his phone. "Let me try him again." He frowns. "Voicemail. Damn. I'm beginning to get concerned now. I hope he's okay. Scott, this is Eli. Call me. It's important."

When Eli places his phone away, I put my arm around his shoulders. "I'm sure there's a simple explanation."

"I've contacted DPS," Morrison tells us. "They're looking for his car on all the roads between here and Austin. If I hear anything, I'll let you know."

WHEN SOLIZ, Morrison, Shaw, and his team drive away, our wonderful neighbors surround Eli. The love and concern they have for him is undeniable.

"Do you see that blue Jeep Wrangler in one of the visitor's parking spots?" Harvey holds out a set of keys for Eli. "It's yours for as long as you need."

"Harvey, that's too much. You didn't have to do that."

"Yes, I did. And enough discussion about it, okay?"

"Okay." Eli takes the keys. "Thank you. I really appreciate this."

Sarah hands me and Eli a sack with some sandwiches and chips inside. "M, made these for you guys—BLTs and potato chips. She knew you would be hungry after this was all over. She'd be here herself but she's watching the baby for Ava."

Ava gives Eli a hug. "I better relieve M of her babysitting duties, but before I go I want you to know that if there is anything at all you need I'll get it for you."

He glances at me. "Thanks for the offer, but I'm in good hands. You all mean the world to me."

Everyone says good-bye and heads back into their own apartments.

I turn to him. "Ready to call it a night?"

"I sure am." As Eli and I walk to my door, he tries to reach Scott again. "Damn it. Where is he?"

I'm starting to wonder if Eli and I are wrong about Scott. Could he have set fire to Eli's car? But if it was Scott, where did he get the SUV that raced away from us near the alley? If it wasn't him, where the hell is he? None of this is making any sense. I wish Eli didn't have to deal with any of this crap. But as long as he does, I plan on being right next to him, giving him whatever support I can.

We step up to my door.

"Well hell, Jackson. In all the confusion with the note I totally forgot to get my things."

I smile. "Don't worry about it. We can get your stuff tomorrow. I've got pajamas you can wear until then."

"It's already tomorrow, Jackson." He grins. "I'm exhausted but there's no way I'm going to be able to fall asleep any time soon."

"Me either." I unlock the door and we walk inside my apartment. "I'm totally wound up."

"Oh, no. Don't you have class?"

I glance at the time on my phone. "Yes, in three hours. But I've made it to class on less sleep."

"You should skip." He kisses me lightly on the lips.

"I might if you take a day off from the station."

"Very tempting. Mm. I think I will."

"Oh really?" I love the back and forth flirtation between us. "You're not even scheduled, are you?"

"You caught me. I don't have to report to the station until day after tomorrow, but I told the captain I would stop by tomorrow morning."

I pull him in close. "You'll never be able to fool me, Eli Grayson. So don't even try."

Setting M's sack on the table, I get us some plates, napkins, and sodas. I start emptying out the contents of the bag and find four chocolate chip cookies. "M thought of everything, Eli."

He sits down at the table. "She did?"

I reach in and pull out the cookies. "Dessert."

I fill our plates and sit next to him.

"I love chocolate chip cookies."

"Me, too. I remember my mom making them for me when I was very young and my dad was still alive."

"So you do have some good memories of her."

"Yes, she was such a great mom until my dad died and she lost the baby."

"I'm sorry that happened to you." He grabs my hand. "Through all of it you have turned out to be such a wonderful, caring man."

"I'm not so wonderful or caring. In fact, I can be a real bastard, as you know already. The second we're done here I will jump up and wash the dishes, wipe the table, and sweep and mop the floor. Thank you, OCD."

"If it bothers you so much, have you ever thought about getting counseling?"

"It's one of the reasons I decided to go into psychology, Eli. I thought I might be able to help myself. Although I understand why I am the way I am I still can't overcome it. That is a puzzle to me. I just don't know why."

"Well, let's think about this. Maybe between the two of us we can figure it out."

"God, you're amazing, Eli Grayson. You care deeper than anyone else I know." I'm glad to have the opportunity to keep his mind off of worrying about Scott. "I'm not sure we can but why not give it a try. How do you want to begin?"

"Do remember when your OCD kicked in?"

"Great question. Have you ever thought about being a psychologist instead of a fireman before?"

"No way, but you're avoiding the question, Jackson. Think back. When did it all start?"

"The first time I noticed it was when I moved into this apartment. The minute I get up in the morning I always make my bed before I do anything else. When I brush my teeth I immediately clean the sink. When I shave I clean it again. I can't stand anything out of place. It drives me crazy, Eli. For instance, do you see that crumb to the left of your plate?"

Eli glances at the tiny spec. "This one?"

"Yes. I'm dying to clean it up but I don't want to be rude."

"Sorry." He knocks it off the table to the floor. "Oh, shit. Jackson, I'm sorry." He takes his napkin and picks the crumb off the floor.

"See, Eli, how difficult I can be."

"This is how you feel now that you have your own place, but how did you feel when you were living with your mom?"

"I cannot begin to explain to you how frustrated I was. Always. Day in and day out. I would try so very hard to get rid of trash but my mom's disease would make her hysterical whenever I took even the smallest thing out. She would go into a total panic attack. So eventually I stopped trying."

"Completely understandable. You were in an awful situation and so young. You were so pent up with frustration with no way to relieve it. I bet that's when your OCD came to life inside you, Jackson, when you were still living at home and totally powerless."

"You're right, Eli. I remember being so embarrassed and ashamed. I told myself over and over that once I had my own place it would be spotless. There would be no dirt or clutter in my house. Ever."

"When you were out of your mother's house, cleaning gave you a sense of control, of power."

"I know. It's still my way of coping. It calms me down when things are difficult to deal with."

"No wonder, like you said before, the pendulum swung the other way after living with her in that house. She was a hoarder and you became the opposite."

"You mean a clean freak?"

"I wouldn't put it that way. You're just a person who needs order in their life." Eli leans forward. "You're working hard to keep your house perfect. You don't want it to ever be like your mother's."

"If I don't, Eli, I will end up just like her. I can't be like her. I just can't." I jump out of my seat and grab a cloth. With tears streaming down my face, I start wiping the counters. The image of my mom on the floor with the box on top of her fills my mind.

He comes up beside me and touches me on the cheek. "This is what you're really afraid of—that you'll become like your mother. That's why you were so adamant to push me away, wasn't it? You're scared that you'll hurt me someday."

"I don't ever want to hurt you." I close my eyes and wrap my arms around him. "I can't be like her. I just can't."

Chapter 17

As my fear continues to bubble up inside me I hold on tight to Eli. "My mom had a breakdown after my dad died and she lost the baby. Who's to say that if something tragic happens to me I won't *snap* just like she did?" Terrified that my past will damage not only me but also him, I let go and step back.

"Please, Jackson. Don't shut me out again."

"I can't risk you having to deal with someone like my mom. I'm her son. I have her DNA. You and I being together is too risky for you, Eli."

"So you've made the decision for me? You're pulling away again?" He shakes his head. "No. That's not happening, Jackson. I'll make my own decision. I get it. I get why you pushed me away so hard after we made love. You're terrified as we get closer you will lose control. You will. So will I. That doesn't mean you're going to end up like your mother did."

"It doesn't mean that I won't either."

He pulls me in close, staring at me with his kind, unblinking eyes. "Sweetheart, even if something happens to you that causes you...how did you say it? That causes you to *snap*, we'll deal with that if and when it happens."

"But what if something happens to you? To us? What if you figure out that you can't love me?"

"Not love you? That's impossible."

"But people break up all the time. Everyone starts relationships believing they will go on forever. Things change. People change. What if we change? What then? What if I go crazy and start hoarding like my mom?"

"You can't live your life fearing the worst. It's not really living, is it? You and I are meant to be together. There's a connection I feel with you that I've never felt with anyone else. And I can tell you feel the same way. That's why you're terrified. Jackson, that's why I'm scared, too. But I'm not giving up on us. Now that I know what you're really afraid of I won't leave again. Push me away a hundred times. I'm going to keep on coming back. I believe in you, in us." He kisses me, wrapping his arms tight around my body.

I feel safe in his arms. Protected. Adored. This is where I belong. With him.

"Sweetheart, together we can conquer anything," he tells me.

"Hearing you say that, I know it's true." I press my lips to his, and he traces mine with his tongue. As our kiss deepens, I feel a wave of desire roll through me. "I need you, Eli, more than I've ever needed anyone in my life."

"And I need you, Jackson." He runs his hands down my arms, and I feel heat swirling inside me. "You're the man I've always dreamed of being with. I want you. So let's hurry and get our dishes washed and put away."

"To hell with the damn dishes. They can wait." I kiss him again. "I can't wait. I'm burning up inside for you. Let's go upstairs."

Eli's eyes sparkle and he smiles broadly. "Jackson, did you hear what you just said?"

"Yes. I heard. I said to leave the mess." I shrug and grin. "Truthfully, I'm surprised at myself. But let's not try to figure out this breakthrough in me right now. Let's head upstairs and get you out of those clothes."

"And you out of yours," he says in a sexy tone that drives me wild.

We race up the stairs to my bedroom, ripping our clothes off and tossing them on the floor. I feel free of my chains and so unbelievably turned on. Totally naked, we jump on the bed together, arm in arm. As our hard cocks touch each other, we kiss ferociously.

Just being next to him completely nude makes my temperature rise and sends sparks down my spine. I could be satisfied if this were all we did, but knowing there is more drives me wild with lust for him.

"Get on your back for me, baby." I watch as he stretches out beside me. He looks like a Greek god from head to toe, ready for me to worship and adore.

Leaning down, I kiss his nipples, first one and then the other, back and forth. The moans that leave his lips thrill me. I want to give him pleasure that will blow his mind. I work my way down, kissing his ripped stomach. I can feel his racing heartbeat through his skin and on my lips. Realizing how much he's enjoying my tender touches raises my desires and the beats of my own heart.

Slowly I move down, coming face to face once again with his beautiful hard cock. I cup his heavy balls and wrap my other hand around his thick shaft.

"Oh God, Jackson. That feels so good."

"You haven't felt anything yet, baby." I swirl my tongue on the tip of his cock, paying extra attention to the slit and the drop of saltiness I taste there.

I continue teasing him this way, raking my tongue up and down his shaft, until he's writhing on the mattress silently begging me for more. "You want more, don't you, sweetheart?"

"Hell, yes. Please. Yes. More."

I swallow all of him until he hits the back of my throat. The loud groan that erupts from him makes me so happy, way beyond anything I've ever experienced before. Pleasuring him thrills me. I suck harder and faster, wanting to give him an orgasm he'll never forget. I tighten my lips and hollow out my cheeks.

He grabs me by the head and tugs on my hair, which only makes me even crazier and causes the pressure inside me to expand and multiply.

"Ohh," he lets out, and I feel his cream hit the back of my throat.

I swallow every drop, clinging to him with both hands.

"Oh my God, Jackson. That was…wow."

"Wow. I agree." I hold him tenderly, feeling his heartbeat slow and his breathing soften.

Once I'm satisfied he's back to normal, I sit up and swing my legs off the mattress. He grabs my hand. "Where do you think you're going?"

"I was going to get dressed," I admit.

He leans forward and pulls me back down. "You're not in charge, sweetheart. Now it's my turn." The forcefulness and heat in his eyes causes my pulse to race and heat up even more. "You're mine, Jackson. All mine."

Holding on to me, he flips both of us around, placing me on my back with him on top of me. He devours my lips and our tongues tangle together. He touches me everywhere with his hands and lips. When he licks my nipples I fist the sheets, overwhelmed with desire and loving every second of it. He clamps down on my nipples with his lips.

I groan loudly. "Feels good. So damn good."

My entire body is out of control. A crushing need races down every vein inside me. As he continues down my body, tracing it with his kisses, an unstoppable want shakes me to my very core. "Please, Eli. I have to have you now."

"Not just yet, baby. But believe me, the wait will be worth it. You'll see." Like I had done to him, he teases my cock with his tongue, driving me wilder.

When he swallows my cock, I feel like I'm on my way to the moon, rocking through space and time. I writhe on the mattress as I feel him tighten his lips around my shaft, bobbing up and down me. I want this to last as long as possible, but I can tell that I won't be able to contain myself.

"Oh fuck." I explode in Eli's mouth, and he drinks down every drop of me.

He moves up, covering my body with his. As he nuzzles my neck, I feel myself getting hard again. I can also feel that he is too.

"I can't seem to get enough of you, sweetheart," he says in a low rumble.

"I feel the same way about you. This isn't just about lust and heat with you. This is intimacy on a level I've never experienced before, Eli," I confess. "Sex has always been about the physical for me. But with you it's so…so…"

"So much more. For me too, baby. You're everything I ever wanted and *so much more.*"

"God, I'm crazy about you." Ready for the next step with him, I open the drawer of my nightstand and retrieve the bottle of lube, a condom, and a hand towel. "I need to feel you inside me. I want the connection."

He stares at the items in my hand. Kissing me tenderly, he whispers, "I need you too." He takes the lube from me.

I roll a condom down his thick cock, and then I flip over on my stomach, placing the hand towel between me and the sheets.

He circles my tight ring with his slicked up hand, which sends heat throughout my body. My balls ache and my cock throbs.

When he pierces my ass with his finger, a spark shoots through me. The initial sting is sharp and causes me to hold my breath for a moment, but immediately after the sting vanishes, all that is left is a deep, powerful hunger for more.

"Oh God, Eli. Please. Make love to me. Please."

He kisses the back of my neck. "Oh yes, sweetheart. That's exactly what I intend to do."

I feel all his weight on top of me, pinning me to the mattress. Feeling his naked body against mine multiplies how much I want him.

"I can't wait any longer. Please. You've got to take me." I press my ass up against his cock.

"Yes, I do, you sexy beast." He gently clamps down on my ear lobe and thrusts slowly into me.

Burning up with desire, I press back into him, taking more of his cock into my body. He pushes deeper into me, and I feel my connection with him tighten and intensify. On many levels we are no longer two but are becoming one, full of passion. He's awakening something very primal and powerful inside me with every stroke.

His thrusts increase in speed. In and out. Over and over. I can't control the moans leaving my lips as I writhe under him, getting closer and closer to the release I so desperately need.

I feel him plunge deep into me in one final stroke, which sends me over the edge and into a mind-blowing orgasm. I shoot into the hand towel just as Eli climaxes inside me.

We remain in this position for several breathless seconds, him on top of me, and then we roll on our sides facing each other.

His phone rings.

Knowing that it could be the police, I say, "You better get that."

"I guess I should." He grabs his phone. "I don't recognize the number. Hello? Scott. Hold on. Let me put you on speaker. Where are you?"

I sit up on the bed, waiting to get the answers we desperately need.

"I just got to the Thompson Center." Scott's voice comes through nice and clear. "They told me that a Detective Morrison has been trying to reach me about another fire that occurred at your apartment complex."

"That's right. What took you so long to get to the center?" Eli asks him firmly. "You should have been there hours ago."

"I hit a deer. I'm okay but my car had to be towed."

"Why didn't you call me?"

"When I hit the deer my soda flew out of the cup holder and soaked my phone. It's totally ruined."

"That explains a lot," I say to Eli.

"Is that Jackson?" Scott asks.

"Yes, it is."

"Tell him I'm sorry how I acted. There's just a lot going on in my life right now."

"It's okay, Scott. I'm just glad you're okay." Remembering how difficult things were for mom to deal with, I feel sympathetic to

Scott's situation. He's trying to get well and I will support his recovery just like Eli is.

"What about this fire the detective wants to speak to me about?"

"Someone set my car on fire last night."

"Oh my God, Eli. Are you okay?"

"I'm fine, Scott." Eli tells him about us driving back from the rodeo and chasing the guy into the alley.

"This Detective Morrison thinks I did it, doesn't he?"

"The police are just checking every possibility," Eli says. "When you talk to Morrison give him the name of the towing company you used. That will settle it once and for all where you are concerned."

"Yes, but it still doesn't explain who burned your place and your car, Eli." Scott's tone is full of concern. "I need to come back."

I'm positive that he is not the arsonist. But who is?

"No, Scott, you don't need to come back to Dallas. You stay in Austin and work on you. I'm fine." With a quick smile, Eli looks at me. "I'm just glad you're okay."

"Do you need to stay at my place until they find the guy responsible?" Scott asks. "It's empty for the next few weeks while I'm here at the center."

"Thanks, but I'm staying with Jackson."

"Jackson again," Scott says in a harsh tone, but in the very next moment he says, "Sorry, Jackson. I'm just…I don't know. I guess I still have to adjust to you and Eli being together."

"It's okay. I get it." No matter how misguided his feelings for Eli are they are still very real to him.

"I appreciate that," Scott says. "Please take care of him. He's a hero, no doubt, but it doesn't keep me from worrying about him."

I grab Eli's hand. "I'll keep him safe, Scott. I promise."

"It's just hard. That's why I'm here. To work on all my feelings. I'll call Detective Morrison when I get off the phone with you guys to verify where I was. I'm calling you from the center's phone right now. They don't want me to have a phone for the first few weeks, so if you need to send me a message you'll have to call this number."

"I'm so glad you're safe," Eli says. "Take care, buddy."

He clicks off the phone and turns to me. "I knew Scott was innocent."

"He definitely isn't the arsonist. I have to admit for a while I thought he was guilty."

"Understandable. It's just that I've known Scott a long time."

"You can see the light in people when others only see darkness." I kiss him. "You're the kind of man I've been longing for my whole life, a man who understands the real me—faults and all. A man who doesn't run away when things get tough but stays."

"Sweetheart, I will never run away. I'm a man who wants you. All of you." He presses his lips to mine. "Jackson, I love you."

"I love you, too." I kiss him.

Chapter 18

Fresh from our shower, Eli and I jump back in the bed and into each other's arms. I gaze into his big blue eyes. "I can't believe how lucky I am to have you."

"You're lucky? I'm the lucky one." He kisses me and I feel desire rise up once again inside me.

My doorbell rings.

"Who could that be at this hour?" I grab my phone. "Damn." I leap from the bed and pull on my jeans, which I had tossed to the floor.

"What's the matter?" Eli asks

"That's Ava. I'm her ride to class."

"Jackson, what time is it?"

"After eight."

"I need to get going too." Eli starts dressing and grabs his phone. "I promised the captain I'd drop by the firehouse this morning, and I need to pick up Vader. I also want to swing by the police station first to make sure Soliz and Morrison understand Scott wasn't responsible for either fire."

I wonder who is responsible but keep that to myself.

Both of us carrying our shoes, we rush down the stairs together. I open the door and Ava walks in.

"Hi, guys." She grins. "Jackson, if you plan on skipping today I can get Trace to take me to class."

"No skipping today. I've got two tests and a lab that I need to make up."

Eli and I sit side by side on the sofa and put on our shoes.

"Mind if I refill my coffee thermos?" she asks.

"Sorry. I didn't have time to make any."

"I see that." She glances at the dirty dishes.

"Oh God, I'm sorry about the mess. Uh. Something came up."

"I can see that." Ava's giggle is endearing and always makes me smile.

Eli and I jump off the couch together.

He hugs Ava. "Have a great day." Then he places his hands on both sides of my face and gives me a kiss. "You too, sweetheart."

Without another word he walks out of my apartment.

"Mm. I *did* interrupt something, didn't I?" Ava grins and hugs me. "I'm so happy for you. You have to swing by Starbucks on the way to school so you can tell me all about it."

"That might make us late to class."

"Not if we hurry. You know I have to have my morning coffee and you didn't make any. Come on, lover boy." She rushes out the door.

AFTER I ANSWER the last question on the test, I take it up to my professor. This one was easier than the earlier test, but I think I aced them both. I get my backpack and walk out of the classroom, anxious to return home. I smile, remembering I still have dirty dishes to deal with.

Since I got out of class early, I'm sure I'll beat Ava to the bench today. Even with the extra time on my side, I speed up my pace to ensure my victory.

"Hey, Jackson."

I turn around and see Brad walking straight for me. *Damn.* "I'm in a bit of a hurry. What do you need?"

"I thought we could go to dinner tonight. My treat. Have you been to the restaurant in Reunion Tower?"

"Brad, I've already told you that we're not a couple and we are not dating."

"I know what you said, Jackson, but what you don't realize is that we are perfect for each other. You just have to give me a chance. That's all I'm asking."

"No chance, Brad. None."

"But—"

"No buts. We're teammates. That's it. Now I have to be going."

He grabs my arm. "Don't rush off. We need to talk."

I jerk my arm free of him. "Damn it, Brad. Leave me alone. Just go."

"I know what this is about." He frowns. "That fucking fireman that lives next door to you. He's gotten into your head and your bed, hasn't he? That creep doesn't hold a candle to me. He can't give you what I can. Can he take you to Europe, all expenses paid? Or anywhere else in the world? Can he buy you a new car? Shower you with expensive gifts? No." Glaring at me, his voice gets louder and louder. "That bastard can't do any of that for you, can he?"

"Get the hell away from me, Brad. I'm sick of this." I turn around and start walking to the bench. I see Ava coming from the other side.

"Jackson," he says behind me. "Don't do this."

Like every other day, Ava starts running to beat me to the bench. Glad to get some distance between me and Brad, I race to meet her. We both reach our meeting place at the same time.

"Jackson, it's a tie today," she says, out of breath. "Don't deny it. You could have beat me if you hadn't been talking to that guy. Oh shit. That's Brad."

"Yes, it is." I glance back at Brad, who is glaring at me but isn't taking a single step our direction. Maybe I got my point across to him after all.

She turns to me. "You okay?"

141

"I am now." I watch as Brad finally turns around and walks away from us in the opposite direction. "That guy is driving me crazy."

"Is he being a little pushy?"

"That's an understatement." I tell her everything Brad said.

"He sounds like a stalker to me. You better be careful." Ava looks concerned. "Jackson, you need to let campus police know about this. I think Adam is on duty. You can tell him about Brad."

"Ava, Brad's just annoying right now. If it escalates, I'll be sure to file a report and a restraining order."

"Fine. But you better promise to be careful with him."

"I promise." On the way to my car, I can't seem to shake the look in Brad's eyes when he was talking about Eli.

Chapter 19

When I pull into my parking spot, Ava and I see Trace and Luke. They're holding the baby and standing by Trace's car.

I turn to her. "What's up with the welcome wagon today?"

"I don't know. Let's find out." She gets out of the car. "Guys?"

"Hey, sweetie," Luke says. "We are going to go to the grocery store. Want to go with us?"

"I better go. Because I remember what happened the last time you two went on your own. We ended up with seven boxes of cereal and a case of beer."

"That's all we need to live on." Trace puts his arm around her. "Jackson, why not join the fun? Maybe we can stop for ice cream on the way back."

"Thanks for the offer, but I've got plans with Eli."

They all smile.

"Don't say a word." I grin. "We're just at the very beginning of our relationship."

"Relationship?" Trace's eyes light up. "That's the best news I've heard in a long time."

"Yep," Ava says. "And they said they were taking it slow. I told you, Jackson, that you would end up in the fast lane with him, didn't I?"

"Sounds like he and Eli are zooming down the love highway to me," Luke says.

"Maybe you're right, and maybe I'm thrilled about it too." I grin. "Just go. I'll talk to you later."

They get in the car and drive away.

At my doorstep, I bend down and grab the newspaper. I know it's weird that I have the paper delivered every day when I could just read the electronic version. But I still like to hold it in my hand when I drink my coffee. Guess I'm a little old fashioned that way.

Just as I unlock my door I get a text from Eli.

"At firehouse. Home in under 30."

Walking inside, I text back, *"Can't wait. Have you had lunch?"*

"Nope. Want me to bring something home?"

"How about we meet at Lucy's Diner?"

"Perfect. Love you."

I smile and type, *"I love you, too."*

I put my phone away, place the paper on the counter, and look at our dirty dishes. Eli might be good for my OCD, but that doesn't mean I can tolerate this mess much longer. I get right to work so I'll have plenty of time to make it to the diner to meet Eli.

Less than fifteen minutes later, the only thing left for me to do is wipe down the counters. As I drag the cloth over the granite a strange feeling makes the hairs on the back of my neck stand up.

I turn around and find Brad standing right behind me.

"What the hell? How did you get in here?"

"Your front door was unlocked."

Reading Eli's text, I must have forgotten to lock it after I got inside. "That didn't give you the right to come in, Brad. What are you doing here?"

"I just...I just had to...make things...Jackson, you know how I feel...I just had to..."

Brad is acting like he's drunk or stoned. So, I say as quietly and in my most non-threatening tone, "Just calm down. Tell me what's on your mind."

"You didn't mean it, did you? You couldn't have meant it."

"Meant what, Brad? What are you talking about?"

"You know what I'm talking about. Us being together."

"I meant what I said, Brad. We're never going to be together."

"Then if I can't have you, no one can." He pulls out a gun from the back of his jeans and points it at my head.

Stunned and fearing the worst, I raise my hands toward the ceiling. "Brad, you don't want to do this."

"We belong together, Jackson. If not in this life, then in the next."

"You're just a little confused."

"Confused? Fuck no. You're confused. Not me." He's having a total breakdown and if I'm not careful he might kill me.

"Haven't you ever heard of the chase?" Looking directly in his eyes instead of at the gun, I plaster a smile on my face, hoping he will buy the lie. "I just wanted you to chase me. That's the fun part."

"Yeah, right. After the way you treated me you expect me to buy your load of crap? I'm too smart for you. Now, do what I say when I say it, Jackson, or this will go very bad for you. Sit in that chair." He motions to one of my dining room table chairs.

"Okay. Just relax. I'll do what you say." My mind is spinning, trying to figure a way out of this mess. All I can do is try to stall him. "Please, let's just talk this out. You've got me all wrong."

"Stop talking. You're confusing me." Keeping the gun pointed at me, he starts rummaging through my cabinets and drawers, tossing everything to the floor.

"What are you looking for?"

"This." He holds up a roll of masking tape, walks over, and tosses it at me. The gun barrel remains fixed in my direction. "Tape your ankles to the chair."

"Okay. Whatever you say." Praying for an escape out of this nightmare, I wrap both my legs to the chair.

"Tighter. I don't want you getting free."

"Sure. But think, Brad. It's not too late to stop this. Will you just listen to me?"

"No. Shut up. I won't listen to your lies. They hurt too much.

You made me fall in love with you. That's your doing. Not mine. I can't stop. I've got to make things right. That's what I'm doing. Yes, it is. We belong together. Yes, we do."

His rambling tells me that he is likely beyond any reach I have. But what else can I do? I can't just give up. So I decide to try once again to convince him that there is a chance for us. Hopefully this time it will calm him down. "Maybe we do belong together, Brad. I'm starting to see that now."

"You are? Really?"

My phone buzzes.

Brad grabs it off the counter. "That fucking fireman. Damn it." He glares at the screen and then throws it to the floor. The screen cracks and the buzzing stops instantly. "Grayson has poisoned your mind against me, hasn't he?"

"No. He hasn't. He has nothing to do with this."

"Bullshit." He punches me in the face. "Oh my God, Jackson. I'm so sorry. I don't want to hurt you."

I taste blood on my lips. "I know you don't. You're just confused."

"Stop telling me I'm confused. You're the one who's mixed up. Not me." The hardness in his face softens for a bit and his tone changes. "But I don't blame you, sweetheart. That's Eli Grayson's fault." Then the hardness returns, horrifically distorting his face. Pounding his fist against his forehead, Brad's next words come out like venom. "He's like a virus, worming his way into your brain." Brad starts pacing in a tight circle right in front of me, lost to his rage. "That fireman has everything to do with this. I've watched that bastard lusting after you. I'm no fool."

This is my opportunity, while he's distracted.

"At the barbeque around your pool, that asshole never left your side."

With my legs constrained, I can't move.

"At your roommate's art show in the courtyard, the same thing. I never got to be alone with you because of him."

My hands are still free, but the only thing within easy reach that I can use as a weapon is the vase. Brad just needs to get a little closer.

146

"At our last tennis match, he fucked you with his eyes from the stands."

Eli was there? Brad saw him but I didn't. That's why Brad put his arm around me and tried to lead me off the court.

"That creep is the reason you are confused. I tried to get him out of your life."

He's still not close enough. "You set his place on fire, didn't you?"

"Of course I did. I did it for us. I hoped the asshole would move away, but instead he ended up moving in with you. My plan should have worked." He pulls out a lighter from his pocket and ignites it, staring at the flame. "Fire is like magic. Power. When I unleash my fiery monster nothing has ever been able to stop it before."

Horrified, I watch Brad pick up the newspaper from my counter. He runs the flame of the lighter under it until it ignites.

He smiles and tosses the burning pages to my sofa, which immediately starts to smolder.

Oh, God. He's going to burn down my apartment with me in it.

Brad grabs one of my kitchen towels and sets it on fire. He throws it on top of the pile of items on the floor that he pulled out of the cabinets and drawers earlier. They ignite instantly.

"I knew I had to try again to make my point with Eli Grayson. So I wrote him a warning in a note and set his car ablaze."

"You did all of that for us?" I can see the flames are spreading from my sofa to the rug. The smoke is building fast. I'm running out of time. "Brad, you're right. You've always been right."

"You really see that now?" He stops and stares at me. "It broke my heart when I saw you that night with him. I wanted to hold you instead of running away down that alley. But you didn't give me a choice."

The temperature is rising fast as the flames multiply. My drapes start to burn and the smoke builds until I can't see the ceiling.

"I'm so sorry, Brad, that I put you through that. I am the one who has been confused." *Get closer. Closer.* "Please, kiss me."

He smiles and leans down.

Closer.

When I can feel Brad's breath on my face, I grab the vase and knock it over his head as hard as I can. He stumbles to the floor and though he's still conscious, I can tell he's dazed. My place is going to be completely engulfed in flames with no way out. No more time to think, only to react. Even though my legs are taped to the chair I lunge for him.

When I land on top of Brad the gun gets knocked out of his hand, bounces on the floor and goes off. I immediately feel a sharp pain in my thigh. I've been hit.

Brad becomes completely enraged and screams, "You lying motherfucker. You're going to pay for this."

He punches me in the face, and I can feel my eye start to swell shut. I try to overpower him with every ounce of strength I have. I have to win this fight if I am to survive. But without the use of my legs I'm unable to keep him from getting away.

Once free of me, Brad gets up on his feet. I can barely see him through the smoke, which is making me cough and burning my eyes. I'm close to passing out from the fumes, but I force myself to stay conscious.

Facing the floor with the chair on top of me, I turn and see Brad, who is also coughing. The flames are all around us. He places his hand over his mouth and with his other hand he grabs the gun and points it at me.

"Why couldn't you love me?" Brad kicks me several times, and I hear my ribs crack. The sudden shock takes my breath from me. I bite my lips and close my eyes, trying to fight against the pain.

This is it. There's nothing else I can do to change the outcome. It's funny what runs through my mind. It's not a rerun of my entire life like some believe happens at this moment. All I see are images of my wonderful fireman. I don't want to leave him. God, why is this happening?

I hear Brad cock the gun and I open my eyes.

He removes his hand from his mouth and an evil, twisted smile appears on Brad's face. "Time to die, sweetheart."

I just can't give up. I have to try. For Eli.

Hoping to trip Brad, I grab his leg and pull. He falls over into the flames and starts screaming.

Frantically, I pull the tape off of my legs. Finally, I'm free of the chair. I try to crawl to the door, but all I see are flames in every direction. The fumes are too strong. I know I'm about to lose consciousness, but I have to get out before I do. I can't seem to make my arms and legs move. *It's too late.*

Through the fogginess of my mind, I hear a voice. Eli's voice.

"Jackson?"

I try to answer but my lips won't move.

"Jackson, I'm here. Hold on."

Hearing sirens getting louder and louder, I feel him lift me off the floor and over his shoulder. Is this real or just a dream? I can't breathe. Everything hurts. My head spins.

All I see is darkness.

Chapter 20

The darkness fades away and I see a pinpoint of light that keeps getting bigger and bigger.

"Jackson? Can you hear me?"

That's Jaris's voice in the distance.

"Jackson, open your eyes for me." Jaris's words pull me out of the fog.

I take a deep breath and start coughing.

"Easy, buddy," Jaris says. "You took in a lot of smoke. That's why the EMTs are giving you oxygen."

I realize I'm lying on a gurney with the head of it raised and I'm wearing an oxygen mask. "Doc, where's Eli? Is he okay?" Anxious, I try to rise up even more to find him.

"Right here, sweetheart." The black ash on Eli's face is a reminder that he risked his life to save me. "I'm fine. Just relax."

"Thank God. I'm so glad you're okay."

"We've got to get you to the hospital to make sure you're going to be fine too."

Jaris nods. "You're doing great, Jackson, but you do have a bullet in your leg that we have to take care of."

I feel more confident knowing that Jaris is taking charge. There's not another doctor I trust more. After working in the ER for so long, nothing seems to rattle him.

Suddenly images of Brad pointing the gun at me burn fresh in my mind. "Where is Brad? He's lost his mind. Someone needs to help him. I think he's on drugs."

"Calm down, baby." Eli squeezes my hand. "I'm so sorry, but Brad didn't make it. I went back in for him, but it was too late."

"Oh my God, I tried to help him, but nothing I did was working."

"It's next to impossible to reach anyone who is high on drugs," Jaris says. "We'll get more answers about him later, but for now, you need to concentrate on your own recovery."

"Yes, Doc. I will. But has anyone notified Brad's family?"

"Detective Soliz is taking care of it," Eli tells me. "Don't worry."

As the EMTs wheel me to the ambulance, I see all my wonderful neighbors. As I look past them, I also see Captain Murphy and his team hosing down the back of my apartment, which has black smoke pouring out of the broken windows. It's clear to me that very little of my things will be saved. But they're just things.

"May I ride in the ambulance?" Eli asks the EMTs.

I look at Eli. He's what matters most to me. "Please. We're together."

"Of course, he can," Jaris tells the EMTs. "I'll meet you at the hospital."

Once they secure the gurney into the ambulance and shut the door, we roll down the road with the sirens blaring.

I see the EMT continuously monitoring my vitals.

Eli never lets go of my hand.

"I never imagined I would be in this position," I tell him. "I'm so glad you're here with me."

"I wouldn't be anywhere else."

We arrive at the hospital. When they get me out of the ambulance, I'm not the least bit surprised to see S & M already waiting for us. They must have left before us to get here so quickly.

"We're going to be right here waiting for you, sweetheart," Martha says with a smile.

"Sir, this is as far as you can go," one of the EMTs tells Eli as two nurses come over to us.

Eli bends down and kisses me on the forehead. "Don't give them any trouble back there, baby. I'll see you when you wake up."

I smile at the man I want to spend the rest of my life with and turn to S & M. "Take care of him for me."

"We will," they say in unison.

"I love you, Eli Grayson."

"I love you, too, Jackson McAllen."

"SO, DOC?" I watch Jaris look over my chart. "Can I go home now?"

Eli shakes his head. "Jackson, you just got out of surgery."

Jaris laughs. "Don't worry. He's not going anywhere until I say so."

"But Doc, it was just a tiny little bullet in my leg. I feel fine."

"I'm glad to hear that, Jackson," Jaris says. "But it was more than just a tiny little bullet hole. We had quite a bit of repairing to do. Otherwise I would have given you a local instead of general anesthesia. You were lucky."

"I know I was." I sigh, remembering all the smoke and flames after taking the shot from Brad's gun.

"I'm keeping you here for at least another day to make sure your lungs are clear. If you give me any trouble, I'll sick S & M on you."

"M and I are right here, Doc, waiting on instructions." Sarah puts her arm around Martha and both look at me with motherly no-nonsense stares.

I grin. "I surrender. You win. I'll stay."

We hear a knock on the door.

"That might be Soliz and Morrison," Eli says. "They want to get your statement."

"It better not be." Jaris turns his attention back to me. "I told them when I saw them in the hallway they had to wait until I felt like you were ready."

"It's fine, Doc. I really want to get this over with."

"You can talk to them but don't sign anything. It isn't wise until you get all the sedation out of your system."

Martha opens the door. "Not the detectives, fellas. It's a delivery guy. More flowers." She takes them from the man. "Thank you."

"Aren't they beautiful," Sarah says.

"Lilies have always been your favorite." Martha holds it up so I can see. A ribbon with the words "Get Well" surrounds the arrangement that also has a tiny tennis racquet ornament.

"Where are you going to put them?" Sarah asks. "I think we've run out of space."

"Don't worry. I'll figure it out. Jackson, these are from your tennis team and coach."

"How nice. I'll have to be sure to thank them. Hey, Jaris, speaking of tennis, when can I get back on the court?"

"You're out this semester, I'm afraid. But you'll be back just like new before too long."

"Oh well. I guess I'll have to take up chess until then."

My hospital room is full of bouquets from my friends. The outpouring of love and support is overwhelming. I'm very grateful that I'm so lucky.

"I'll be back later today to check on you." Jaris walks to the door just as Aunt Jenny walks in with coffee for everyone. "Hello, Mrs. Hall."

"I told you, Doctor, to call me Jenny."

"You got a deal if you'll call me Jaris."

She smiles. "Deal. How's my nephew?"

"He's doing extremely well. We're going to keep him overnight as a precaution, but I'll have him out of here by tomorrow."

"That's the best news I've heard today. Thank you for taking such good care of Jackson."

"It isn't easy with a stubborn guy like him." He looks at me and winks.

We all laugh.

Aunt Jenny hands the coffees to everyone and comes over to my bed. She leans over and gives me a kiss on the cheek. "You'll do what Jaris says, Jackson. No arguments."

I smile. "Yes, ma'am."

"You sure you're ready to talk to the detectives?" Jaris asks me.

"I am."

"I'll send them in." He leaves.

"Why don't we take these coffees and stretch our legs, ladies?" Aunt Jenny asks. "They'll be too many in this room."

"Totally agree with you." Sarah grabs her purse.

"Eli, if you or Jackson needs us just call my cell." Aunt Jenny holds up her phone.

"I sure will."

Aunt Jenny and S & M walk out of the room.

Eli comes over to the side of my bed. "I better do this while the coast is clear." He leans down and presses his lips to mine. "I love you, Jackson McAllen. Don't you ever scare me like that again."

"I love you, Eli Grayson." Grinning, I touch his face. "I thought it would be best to get all the tragedies over with right at the start. That way the rest of our lives will be smooth sailing."

The door opens and Soliz and Morrison walk in.

"Glad to see you're doing so well after all you've been through, Mr. McAllen," Soliz says.

"I'm glad too."

"This shouldn't take too long." Morrison pulls out a notepad. "We just have a few questions for you. The rest we can get from you later."

It only takes a few minutes to answer their questions. They mainly want to find out what my relationship was to Brad.

"Even though I told him several times that we could only be friends, he just wouldn't hear it. He wanted more than I was willing to give."

Morrison turns to Soliz. "Same thing happened in Chicago when he fixated on his next door neighbor."

She nods.

"Brad's done this before?" I ask.

"It's a pattern of his," Soliz tells me. "After we identified him from the print on Eli's car, we looked into his record. He's been in trouble with the law for years. Arson, drugs, and stalking. Quite the record."

"How the hell did he get into the university with a record like that?" Eli asks.

"His parents, that's how," Morrison states flatly. "That's why his parents helped him move to Dallas, to get out of hot water. Every time Brad got in trouble they would bail him out and make things better. Money talks."

"Yes, but it doesn't fix everything," Soliz adds. "Now they've lost their son. We've already placed Brad at the scene of two of the other fires in Oak Lawn and believe he likely was responsible for the rest of them."

"I think we have all we need from you today." Morrison puts his notepad away. "If we have any more questions we'll contact you."

"Thank you, Jackson," Soliz says. "Feel better."

She and Morrison walk out the door.

I look at Eli. "Damn, I had no idea Brad was so ill. If I'd known maybe I could have helped him."

"Don't blame yourself, sweetheart." Eli grabs my hand. "You tried, but some people can't be helped, especially when they are abusing drugs."

"When people have mental illness they really don't know what to do. Maybe Brad was taking drugs just trying to feel normal."

"You have the biggest heart I've ever known," Eli says. "You've already forgiven him. It may take me a little longer. I almost lost you."

"But you didn't lose me." I smile. "You came into that blaze and carried me out. You're a flesh and blood hero. My hero."

"Stop it." He grins and then kisses me.

Chapter 21

E li drives me from the hospital back to Mockingbird Place in my Nissan.

"I'll have to be sure to thank Trace for helping me get your car to the hospital." Eli turns on to Lemmon Avenue.

"He's a great friend. I've always been able to depend on him."

"Trace was so happy that you are going to be staying with me. I think he's almost as excited about it as I am."

"That crazy guy has wanted me to get hooked up ever since he fell in love with Luke." I smile. "I'm excited about staying with you, too, sweetheart." I glance over my shoulder at the crutches in the backseat. "But I hate that I'm going to be so much trouble."

"Honey, you've got to be kidding. Look what you did for me when I needed you. But more importantly, I've wanted you to be with me for so long and now it's finally happening. A dream come true. I wish it was under better circumstances, but I'm thrilled you will be staying with me."

"I don't deserve you, sweetheart, but I'm so glad I have you in my life." I lean over and kiss him on the cheek, and out of the corner of my eye I notice those damn crutches again. "I can't believe Jaris says I have to use crutches until our next appointment."

"We don't want your wound to start bleeding if you put any weight on your leg. You'll get used to it. And if you don't, I'll be happy to carry you wherever you need to go."

"I'm a pretty big guy, you know. But I will take your assistance going up and down the stairs."

When he turns into the parking lot, I see that all the windows on the back of my apartment have been boarded up.

"Before we go to your place, do you mind if we look at mine?"

"Of course I don't mind. I know exactly how you feel." He pulls into my parking space.

He gets out and walks around to my side. He grabs the crutches and hands them to me. I'm a little shaky at first as I exit the car, but with his help I quickly get steady.

He keeps his arm around me as we walk up to my patio gate. Before we walk inside, I notice some of Unit E's windows are also boarded up.

"Oh my God, Eli. Did the fire spread to Trace and Luke's place? Ava and the baby are okay, aren't they?"

"Everyone is fine. They were at the grocery store when Brad showed up at your place."

I breathe a sigh of relief. "I remember. Thank God."

"They got some damage, a little fire but mostly smoke. They're all staying at Harrison's house until it gets fixed."

"Damn, probably everything in their place smells like smoke and that won't be good for the baby."

"Harvey says it will be as good as new when they move back."

"I know it will, I just hate that they're going through the inconvenience of having to leave."

"You know, sweetheart. Things happen for a reason. And all I'm going to say is, you should have seen the grin on Harrison's face." Eli opens the gate, and we walk onto my patio.

Once inside the apartment, I see my wonderful neighbors are hard at work to get it back to normal. The unit has already been cleared of all the debris and now they've started painting it.

Tony and Stephen are working in the kitchen together. I would have never guessed them to become close. They are so opposite of each other. Is it romance or just friendship? I just don't know.

Harvey, Adam, and Oliver are putting in a new front door. S & M are taping the new drywall in the living room.

Tony spots us first. "Hey, everybody. Look who's here."

They all stop what they're doing and rush over to us.

"You look so good, Jackson," Stephen says.

Tony hands me a bottle of beer. "You can drink beer now, right?"

"I don't know why not. It's just my leg. Thanks, buddy." I take a sip. "Mm. Just what the doctor ordered, but don't tell Jaris I said that."

They all laugh.

"Here," Oliver says, pushing a folding chair next to me. "Take a load off."

"Thanks." I sit down. "I appreciate all of you and what you're doing for me. It's weird seeing my place like this without any of my stuff."

Martha bends down and kisses me. "Don't you worry about a thing. We were able to save some of your stuff that was upstairs. And what we weren't, the insurance is going to replace."

"The good thing is we found a metal box full of photos in your closet that survived the fire," Harvey says.

"Oh, thank God. Those were the only pictures I have of my mom and dad. They couldn't have been replaced."

Harvey nods. "We gave them to your aunt for safe keeping."

I'm overwhelmed at the outpouring of love and concern. Feeling my eyes well up, I take a long drink from the bottle, hoping to keep my composure.

"I knew it," Jaris says, walking in the back door. "Jackson, I knew I would find you here. And look at you. Less than an hour from being released and you're drinking beer." He laughs. "But seriously, you need your rest."

"It has been a long day, Doc," I admit, feeling the fatigue creeping in.

Eli helps me to my feet.

"Don't worry about dinner tonight, boys," Martha tells us. "S and I have that covered for you."

"Chicken and dumplings and apple pie." Sarah kisses me on the cheek. "You get out of here and get some rest. We'll drop it off later."

Eli and I walk out the front, and my neighbors get right back to work.

It takes some effort to get up the stairs at his place, but with his help I'm able to manage it. Once on the bed, he stretches out next to me.

"I'm so glad you're here, Jackson. I can't tell you how happy it makes me."

I look into his beautiful blue eyes. "You can say that after all the trouble it took to get me up the stairs and into bed? Wait until you have to help me take a shower. Then we'll see if you feel the same way."

"There is nothing that will change the way I feel about you, sweetheart." He tenderly presses his lips to mine and softly says, "Jackson, I was going to wait to talk to you about this, but I can't wait. I want you to stay with me forever. I'm so in love with you I can't imagine spending even a single day without you." He kisses me deeply before I can respond.

"I love you so much. Yes. I want to be with you forever too, sweetheart."

Another kiss, and we wrap our arms around each other. We stay in that position, enjoying the feeling of being together.

Chapter 22

E li Grayson – six weeks later.

I PUT the food down for Vader and Snow. "Here you go, you two."

They hurry past me to their bowls. The two cats are getting along so well.

Not sure how long Scott will be at the Thompson Center, but I know it's going to be hard to let Vader go back home with him when he returns to Dallas. Hard on me and hard on Jackson. But I bet Scott will let us keep Vader overnight sometimes.

I was surprised when Jackson decided to make Snow our pet, especially with his OCD. He first got attached to Vader and then quickly realized that it's quite nice to have a pet in the house. While Jackson was still on the crutches, we would sit outside on my patio whenever the weather was nice. Snow kept meeting us there, likely because she was curious about Vader, but also because she had become attached to Jackson. And that little cat won his heart. I'm not sure who tamed whom. We took Snow to the vet to get her shots and to make sure she couldn't have any babies.

Jackson and I are all settled in together with these two silly cats, just like one big happy family. He's not moving back to his old apartment. We're staying here in Unit C. With the insurance money, we've picked out all the new furniture together. It was so much fun decorating it, and the apartment really feels like *our* home now.

Jackson comes down the stairs wearing jeans, a Western shirt, boots, and cowboy hat, which have become one of his favorite outfits. "Hey, baby."

"Hey, yourself, handsome."

We kiss.

"How's the leg feeling today?"

"Just like new. Doc was right." He kisses me and bends down to pet Vader and Snow. "I thought we could go dancing after we finish the walk-through with Harvey today at mom's house. What do you say?"

I grin. "I say yes, as long as you don't overdo it."

"You know Jaris has released me."

I put my hands on his shoulder. "Jaris may have, but I haven't given mine yet."

"You worry too much about me, Eli Grayson."

"Yep, and that's never going to change. How much time do I have before we need to leave?" I ask him. "I'd like to grab a quick shower before we go if I can."

He wraps his arms around me. "You have plenty of time, sweetheart. That is if I can let you go."

"God, I love you." I kiss him. "But we don't want to be late."

"I love you, too." He releases me and pours himself a cup of coffee. "Eli, I can't believe this day is already here. Harvey is truly a magician with his tool belt."

"A tool belt and some great subcontractors. But he did finish the job at your mom's house really fast."

"I wonder what it looks like."

"Well, we're about to find out. I'll hurry." I rush up the stairs to the bathroom, and am shocked to see Jackson hasn't wiped down the sink. I smile. His OCD is getting better and better every day.

After my shower, I put on my jeans, boots, Western shirt, and cowboy hat, and then I head downstairs.

"Wow, you look hot," he says. "I'm not sure I should let you out of this apartment looking that good."

"Me? Have you seen yourself in the mirror?" I pull him in close. "One more kiss and then we have to go."

"Deal." He presses his lips to mine, making me wish we could reschedule today's appointment.

But this is too important a day for Jackson. This will be the first time I've seen his mother's home, and the first time he's seen it since Harvey finished the remodeling. I hope that this will help heal the painful memories he has associated with that house.

We walk out the back door to my new Honda Pilot. I've had it for a month now but it still has that new car smell. Jackson helped me pick it out, and I love it. It's the perfect size for us, especially since we had to buy so many things for the apartment.

As I pull out of Mockingbird Place's parking lot, Jackson connects his phone to the car's radio. "Since we're going to the Roundup, how about we listen to Luke Bryan on the way to mom's house?"

"Perfect."

We like all kinds of music, but our favorite is country, especially since we both like to line dance and two-step. We both sing to the music, though neither of us are very good, but you would never know it by the enthusiastic way we belt out the notes.

I turn the corner and we see everyone is already waiting on us. "Are we late?"

"No." He grabs my hand. "They're early, but can you blame them? This is exciting. It looks so good. Harvey even planted some new shrubs and flowers."

"The house is the best looking one on the block, baby."

It's a mid-century brick home with big windows and a red door.

"Sweetheart, this may sound crazy but I'm a little anxious to see the inside. I hope Elisa will like it."

She and her son Jason are on the porch talking with Harvey and his boyfriend Nathan.

"I'm sure she will, and so will you. You ready, sweetheart?"

He nods, and we get out of the Pilot.

Jason spots us first and comes running, yelling, "Unkey Lee-Lee. Unkey Jack. You're here."

He jumps up in my arms. "Hey, sweetie."

I throw him in the air to Jackson. Jason screams with delight.

He has spent the night with us a few times when Elisa had to work an overnight shift. That's when Jackson came up with the idea of renting his mother's house to Elisa instead of selling it.

I'll never forget the smile on his face when he told me what he wanted to do.

"Eli, it's a win-win. Elisa gets cheaper rent and I get a steady income that can help pay for grad school. But the biggest plus is she won't have to work overnights any more. I want to make it clear to Elisa that we still want him to spend the night with us sometimes."

"Can I see my house now, Unkey Jack?" Jason asks him.

Jackson smiles. "You sure can. We all can. Let's go."

We walk up to Elisa, Harvey, and Nathan, shaking their hands.

The very first step inside welcomes us with its warm tones and soft furnishings. The hardwood floors run through the entire space.

I can tell by the look on Jackson's face that he is overwhelmed and thrilled.

He turns to Harvey. "Oh my God. This place is beautiful. I never imagined this could be so stunning. How did you...it's more than...you did this."

"I did," he says with a smile. "I'm so glad you're pleased."

"Pleased? It's perfect. Don't you think it's perfect, Elisa?"

She wipes her eyes. "Yes. Perfect. You can't rent this to me, Jackson. It's worth so much more than you're asking. I can't afford what you could get for it."

He hugs her. "I can rent it to you and I will. You can't just trust anyone these days. And you and Jason are family. That's worth so much more than money."

"Where's my room, mommy?"

"I'm not sure," she says.

Harvey takes Jason's hand. "Let me and Nathan take him to his room while you look at the rest of the house. Nathan and I painted race cars on his walls."

"Please, mommy. Please. Can Unkey Harbey take me?"

She smiles. "Sure he can."

Harvey and Nathan take Jason down the hall.

"Look at the fireplace," Elisa says. "I love the white stacked stones."

"Gorgeous," Jackson says. "I turned Oliver loose for all the decorating. Elisa, do you like the furniture he chose?"

She hugs him and kisses his cheek. "I love everything about it. Everything. I want to take a look at the kitchen."

He smiles. "Knock yourself out. We're right behind you."

She rushes into the kitchen, which has white cabinets, dark granite counters, a large island, and stainless steel appliances. "This is too good to be true."

Jackson takes my hand, and whispers, "This *is* too good to be true. I don't know how to express what I'm feeling right now."

"You don't have to, sweetheart."

He turns to me. "But I do. Knowing Elisa and Jason will be creating new memories in my mom's home, this beautiful home, makes me so happy. And you, Eli Grayson, are the reason I have my life back. Hell, you are my life, my happiness. I love you so much."

I kiss him. "You are my life, too, Jackson McAllen. You are my happiness. I love you."

Chapter 23

r. Jaris Black – six months later.

I LOOK at the time on my phone. Ten minutes left on this shift.

"Here you go, Jaris." Sam, the head ER nurse hands me a cup of coffee.

I take a sip. "Perfect. I sure need this. Thanks."

Sam and I have worked together for a long time. He and his husband Ted have two boys, ages five and six. They're living the dream. "I'm sure glad it's finally quieted down. It's been a long shift, hasn't it?"

"It sure has, but thankfully it's almost over. And I have the wedding shower in about an hour."

"For your friends Eli and Jackson?"

"Yes, but it actually has turned into a double wedding. Do you remember meeting Ava and Harrison at my birthday party?"

"Oh, yeah. They live with Trace and Luke and little Mick."

"That's the ones. I was afraid that the five of them would leave

Mockingbird Place one day, but they didn't. After the fire, Jackson moved in with Eli because his unit had to be gutted."

Sam shakes his head. "What a nightmare all those fires were. I'm glad that's over."

"Me, too. That's when Ava and Harrison convinced S & M to take Jackson's old apartment and the one she, Trace, and Luke had been currently living in and completely redo them. They made the two units into one big place with four bedrooms, two and a half baths, a huge kitchen and dining room. The other half bath they turned into a gorgeous laundry room."

"Sounds like quite the place. I remember you telling me about how afraid Trace and Luke were when Ava started dating Harrison."

"Yeah. The guys were afraid they would lose the baby if Harrison and Ava got serious. Well, they were wrong. Harrison and Ava are getting married, and the five of them are one big happy family living together."

Sam grins. "That's got to be the luckiest little kid in the world."

"He sure is. Did I tell you that Mockingbird Place has a new baby?"

"Only a few times this shift. A hundred times previous shifts." He laughs. "Lashaya and Hayden's baby. Alison Marie."

I grin. "I guess I have talked about it."

"I love it. Don't ever stop, Jaris. I've only been around your neighbors once or twice but I feel like I know them. They're like family to you."

"They sure are."

"If there is ever a vacancy, please let me know. I want to bring Ted with me to look. I think living there would be amazing, especially for our boys."

"I sure will let you know. You guys would fit in perfectly. Oh, good. There's Dr. Glover. I can go now. See you next week, Sam."

"Have fun, Jaris. You deserve it."

"I believe I do. Hopefully I won't get called back for some emergency."

"Fingers crossed."

"Fingers crossed." I rush out to my car.

Once at my place, I head upstairs to the bathroom to get ready for the pool party.

Sporting my favorite red trunks, I look at my reflection in the mirror. "Not bad, Dr. Black. Maybe you'll find a special someone at the pool today." I sigh. It's been ages since I've been in a relationship. It was back in medical school, and that didn't work out. In fact, it ended badly.

God, I haven't thought of Maddox in years.

Why am I trying to lie to myself? No one is here but me. The man ripped my heart to pieces, and I think about him all the time.

"This isn't about you today, Jaris." I grab a towel, head down my stairs and out the door to join the party.

Chad, who lives with Josh next door, comes up with a tray of multicolored shots that match his hair, which is no surprise to me. He's our resident bundle of joy. A true unique spirit. "Doc, would you like a Jell-O shot?"

"Sure. Why not?" I take a blue one. "Sorry I missed your last gig."

"No worries. You're a doctor. You have important work to do. I'm just a musician, and Red Shimmer has lots of gigs coming up that you can come to. Besides, Frankie, Josh, and I are going to play a few songs today."

"Awesome. I see one of the happy couples is already in the pool."

Laughing hysterically, Eli and Jackson are splashing each other with water guns. God, they are so in love. I'm so happy for them.

I watch all the other people who are more than just neighbors to me having fun. "Chad, look at Ava and Harrison sitting on the bench under Malcolm's tree."

He smiles. "It's easy to see how much they mean to each other. Are they even aware that the rest of us are here?"

"I doubt it. And take a look at who's on the blanket next to them —Trace and Luke playing with my little nephew."

"My little nephew, too. You know I've been told he looks like me."

"Oh, really? By who?" I grin. "Maybe someone in your dreams?"

"Maybe so." Chad puts his hand on my shoulder. "Hey, just because you got to deliver the little guy doesn't mean you are a better uncle than me."

"You know that man in your dreams? He told me I was."

We laugh.

"I never thought I'd be crazy about babies, but honestly, Jaris, I'm nuts about our two angels." He points at the baby, who is sitting on Lashaya's lap. "Do you like the swimsuit I bought for our sweet baby Alison? Lashaya and Hayden love it, that's why they put it on her for the party today."

"Well, I have to admit it's the first baby tie-dye swimsuit I've ever seen."

"I know. One of a kind. Gorgeous." Chad smiles. "Just like Alison."

"She is a doll." I get a whiff of the food on the grill. "That smells so good."

"I have no doubt it's going to be delicious since S & M are barbequing."

"Oh my God, Chad. Is that Scott walking up?"

"It looks like him. What the hell is he doing here?"

"I wonder if Eli and Jackson see him?" My gut tightens when I see them getting out of the pool, heading toward Scott. "Apparently they do."

"Jaris, I think we better go over there in case there is a problem. We don't want their day ruined."

"I agree."

When we get to them, Eli puts his arm around Scott.

Scott laughs. "Eli, you're getting me wet."

"So? I'm just very happy to see you. I had no idea you were going to make it."

"The center gave me the green light. I'm a new man."

Jackson shakes his hand. "I'm so glad you're here. You look great."

"Thanks. You look great too. Congratulations. This is for you,

Jackson." Scott hands him a gift and then he hands another one to Eli. "I am so happy for you both. Eli, I haven't felt this good since my parents died. I feel like my old self again."

Seems everything is okay between these three, and I feel my shoulders relax.

My phone rings.

I turn to Chad. "I hope this isn't an emergency I have to deal with at the hospital. I'm ready to have some fun."

"Tell them you're sick and can't make it, Doc."

"I wish I could." I step to the side, shade the screen with my hand so I can see the number. I don't recognize it. "Hello, this is Dr. Black."

"Jaris, this is Maddox."

About the Author

Lee Swift, who writes under several pen names including Kris Cook, creates novels, short stories, screenplays and more.

With an unquenchable thirst to experience all his life journey has to offer, Lee and hubby love travel but still call Dallas, Texas home.

Join [HERE] to get updates on Lee.

Also by Lee Swift

Novels

Morvicti Blood *(Supernatural Thriller)*

Cupid's Arrow *(Gay Fantasy Romance)*

Three to Play *(Menage MMF Romance)*

(All series listed in best reading order)

Mockingbird Place

(Gay Romance Series)

The Marine in Unit A

The Cowboy in Unit E

The Fireman in Unit C

The Doctor in Unit H

The Fighter in Unit J

Holiday Beaus (Novella)

The Musician in Unit G

The Cop in Unit B

Wolf Pack

(Menage MFM Romance Trilogy)

Secret Cravings

Primal Desires

Delicious Hunger

Eternal Trio Series

(Gay Menage Fantasy Romance)

Levi's Rogues

Perfection

Writing with Lana Lynn
(Thrillers)

Lexi's Protector *(Men Without A Cause)*

Liz's Guardian *(Men Without A Cause)*

Secret Diary Series as Kris Cook
(Erotic Straight BDSM Trilogy)

Mia's Spanking Diary

Misty's Bondage Diary

Lea's Ménage Diary